Evil

WOL-VRIEY

Other Books By Wol-vriey:

The Bizarro Story of I
Meat Suitcase
Chainsaw Cop Corpse
Vegan Zombie Apocalypse
Boston Posh (Bud Malone #1)
Vegan Vampire Vaginas
Vagina Mundi
Melanie Nemesis Catchpole
Bizarro 101: A Basic Primer
Boston Corpse (Bud Malone #2)
Dr. Orgasm
Boston Lust (Bud Malone #3)
Pussy Transmission
Hell Dancer
Girls Are Not Smiling
Brainchew
Brainchew 2: Out of Their Heads
Blue Nightmares
Daria (An Erotic Nightmare)
Wet Bones
Mr. Ugly
Brutal

Novellas and Short Stories By Wol-vriey

Big Trouble in Little Ass
Forever Ago Sunshine

Evil

WOL-VRIEY

Burning Bulb
PUBLISHING

Evil
By **Wol-vriey**

Burning Bulb Publishing
P.O. Box 4721
Bridgeport, WV 26330-4721
United States of America
www.BurningBulbPublishing.com

Cover artwork by Anton Rosovsky.
Author Photo: Lolade Akinsowon © 2014.

First Edition.

Paperback Edition ISBN: 978-1-948278-12-6

Printed in the United States of America

CHAPTER 1

Ronan

The evil began on a warm Saturday evening in mid-August, a week before Sylvia Stewart's 30th birthday party.

Out in the large barn amidst the sunflowers, Ronan Higgins stared down in disbelief at his dead daughter. He stood beside Cathy's corpse and wondered how it had happened. He stared while his body trembled uncontrollably from a cold internal wind.

All he'd asked Cathy to do was fetch him his old chainsaw. The chainsaw was out in this barn because they hadn't used it in ages. Sometimes the damn thing didn't start. Ronan had since replaced it with a new model. But this evening, the new one had quit working while he'd been cutting a log and he'd decided to see if the old one would work again.

Cathy had just had to walk out here through the blooming sunflower fields, pick the chainsaw up off the workbench, and bring it back over to him in the first barn.

And so, how the hell did she . . . ?

At the moment Cathy Higgins had a pickaxe blade through her head. Emerging amidst a mess of blood, the metal axe spike was sticking out of her right eye. Six inches of metal, the pistil of a morbid red flower, one with shattered bone as its petals. The spike hadn't punctured her eye though, it had just shoved it out of place. The displaced eye was now wedged between her nose and the reddened metal.

Cathy lay on her back on the barn floor, her torso slightly raised by the axe handle. The pickaxe's other spike was fully stuck into the ground beneath her head. Her blonde hair was floral with blood. Her mouth had a surprised expression. So did her undisplaced left eye, which was wide open and staring at nothing.

Ronan knew what had happened: his daughter had somehow tripped and fallen backwards on the axe, which he'd left stuck in the barn floor at a spot where a slab of the concrete flooring had been removed. Gravity had done the rest—killed her and rammed the pickaxe head all the way into the ground.

After a while Ronan's shock gave way to tears. *Oh, my baby girl. What have I done to you? This is all my fault.* He'd not wept in years, but now his body shook as waves of intense sorrow overcame him.

***

Ronan Higgins, proprietor of Higgins Farms, was a dark, tall and muscular man in his late forties. His 19-year-old daughter Cathy was everything to him. His wife Lisa had died five years ago. Since then, Cathy had been the center of his life.

And now this . . . he stared down at his little girl, lying there with the pickaxe spike jutting from her face like a unicorn's horn. The flow of tears increased until his vision blurred.

Ronan didn't blame anyone but himself for Cathy's death. He clearly remembered leaving the pickaxe stuck here in the earth a month or so ago. They rarely used this old barn now and it had seemed safe enough.

Just as it had seemed safe to send the dead girl out here.

***

Finally, Ronan got some control over himself. The tears were still streaming down his cheeks but he could function. He knelt and with trembling fingers tried pulling Cathy's head off the axe head. However, he couldn't stand the horrible feeling of holding her dead flesh, or the feel of her bloody hair on his forearms. So he quit, stood up, wiped his hands off, and pulled out his cellphone instead.

He dialed 911 but got no response. No "The number you have called cannot be reached at this time," or "This subscriber has been disconnected or is no longer in service," or other intercept message. Nothing. All Ronan heard was a soft hum, like there was a refrigerator working on the other end of the line.

He walked over to the barn door and redialed. Out across the planted fields, he could see two phone towers which served the town of Chester. So he should have a signal. But there still wasn't any.

Ronan scowled at the phone. *Maybe the damn thing's busted.*

He wiped his eyes dry. Then, after a look back at Cathy's corpse which almost started him crying again, he set off for the distant farmhouse. He'd call from the landline instead.

***

Ronan ran through the sunflower field. Normally, being amidst the tall plants with their large radiant blooms cheered him up. Now he didn't even notice them.

He reached the farmhouse. He was panting, out of breath.

He and Cathy were the only ones living on the farm. Ronan had two fulltime farmhands, a married couple named Jerry and Donna Bancroft. He hired other farm help as occasion demanded. The Bancrofts lived in the nearby town of Chester, which was just down State Route 20. They'd driven off for home an hour ago.

The farmhouse phone wasn't working either. On a normal day, this weird coincidence would have perplexed Ronan. Now he ignored it— a small bother consumed by a big one—and stepped outside again. He hurried over to his old white pickup truck, climbed in, and started up the engine.

I'd best just drive into town and report her death.

Action was helping him cope. He put the pickup truck in gear and rolled off down the road.

Ronan's farm lay just off Route 20, about twenty miles in from the west Massachusetts border. Twenty acres of farmland, five of that dedicated to sunflowers, and with a pond too. He also raised sheep and had a few pigs. The more distant farm acreage was cultivated with potatoes and corn. All in all, it was a profitable venture.

While not actually isolated, the farmhouse was situated somewhere in the middle of the acreage, with access to the highway via a long and winding gravel and dirt road half a mile long. If not paying close attention, it was possible to miss the Route 20 turnoff to Ronan's house. The gravel road had a border of trees. On nearing the highway, these trees thickened into full-fledged woodlands.

As Ronan sped towards the highway, inane thoughts flowed through his mind. He made no attempt to stem them. He welcomed any distraction. Anything to deflect the pain beginning to take deep root in his heart. Cathy's death was still inconceivable to Ronan. It was the worst possible thing that could happen to him—his only child dying. And in such an awful fashion.

So he let himself think on other things. Nice and normal everyday things.

I'll need to call Sylvia and let her know her party's off. Sylvia was Ronan's niece, his older sister's daughter. She'd be thirty next Saturday and was planning to hold a huge disco bash at the farm, complete with a celebrity DJ.

Sorry, girl, Ronan thought, *but I can't have you making all that noise during this mourning period. Damn, but Cathy was so looking forward to that party!*

It was another reminder of what he'd been unable to forget anyway.

It was at this moment that Ronan turned a bend in the road and almost ran into the man in black.

CHAPTER 2

The Man in the Road

Ronan stomped the brake hard, just in the nick of time. The pickup truck skidded left, but missed the man. Its rear end seemed to rear up and pitch Ronan forward towards the windshield. He hit the steering wheel then fell back into his seat again.

Foot firmly on the brake, Ronan sat there with his eyes closed, trying to calm his breathing. He didn't need this nonsense. Not today of all days when he'd just left his only kid back there with a metal spike through her head.

I damn near almost killed that guy! Why is he walking in the middle of the damn road!?

"Hey, you okay, man?"

Ronan opened his eyes. The man he'd almost killed was standing by the pickup truck, right by Ronan's door. He was bent over and leaning in the window.

Anger welled up in Ronan. "Dude, can't you watch the hell where you're going!?"

"Are you okay, Ronan?" the man asked again. "I didn't mean to startle you, but I didn't want you driving past me in your hurry to tell the police about your daughter's death."

"Huh?" Ronan gaped at the man. "How'd you know . . . ?"

"I know many things, Ronan," the man in black said. He grinned, revealing large teeth. "You and me, we need to have a little talk."

Ronan now got a proper look at the man. And right off the bat, that proper look alarmed Ronan. Mainly because, even bent over as he was, the man's waist was at the height of the pickup truck window.

Which means he's got to be at least eight or nine feet tall!

That aside, the man's face was old and well-creased. If asked to guess at his ethnicity, Ronan would have said 'Mexican,' because his

5

long dark hair and black eyes gave him the air of a shaman. But no, he wasn't exactly Latino. His eyes seemed to know everything. He had very large hands, but on a second consideration, Ronan decided his hands were merely proportionate to the rest of him. In addition to his black suit, he was also wearing a black cowboy hat. His voice was as raspy as a great-grandfather's and yet possessed a low silkiness to it as if he'd once been a country and western singer.

But how the hell can he be so damn tall? Tall and skinny, like some tree come to life?

Ronan peered beyond the tall man, at the trees, glistening fresh with drops of late summer rain on their leaves. He wished he was away from here, already in town and telling the story of his immense loss to the police. Once that was done he could shut down and grieve, knowing the cops were tidying things up for him, knowing someone else was helping him bear his huge horrible burden.

As far as his companion was concerned, Ronan finally decided he was just seeing and hearing things. His sorrow must have seeped in deeper that he'd thought.

My baby girl just died and I'm hallucinating. This giant guy ain't even really here. I need to watch it or I'll go crazy!

"You're not hallucinating, Ronan," the man said as though reading his mind. "I'm here in the flesh. And like I say, we gotta talk."

Ronan looked the giant in the face. "C'mon, dude. I'm not gonna ask you how you know my daughter's dead, but since you do know that, then you must know too that I can't hang around here yapping with you." He frowned. "Look, I gotta go . . ."

"It's about Cathy that we must talk, Ronan. How would you like to have her back alive again?"

Ronan began feeling annoyed. He scowled at the giant standing by the truck. "Alive? Are you psycho? My daughter has a pickaxe spike through her head. Her brains have leaked out on the barn floor and you're joking about it?"

"I'm not joking, Ronan. I'll make you a deal—I'll bring Cathy back to you, but in return you have to do something for me. What do you say to that?"

Ronan was now beside himself with rage. "Screw you, man," he spat at the giant, whose face had remained impassive since they'd begun this surreal conversation. In fact, the man seemed so calm, he could be part of the surrounding woods.

Ronan decided the tall man was crazy and possibly dangerous. He'd mention the guy to the Chester cops and let them deal with him.

"Bye, dude, I gotta go!"

Ronan took his foot off the brake and stomped on the gas pedal instead. But instead of the pickup truck moving forward, its engine stalled.

Huh?

Ronan turned the starter key again. The pickup's engine sputtered back to life. The moment he tried to roll forward though, the engine quit once more. A third attempt produced the same result.

"Until I say so, it will only roll backward," the man in black said. "Try it if you don't believe me."

Ronan was tempted to put the truck in reverse. But then, he had a sudden conviction that his unwelcome companion *wasn't* lying. This assurance was as sharp and as frightening as being stabbed in the belly with a knife.

He sighed at the giant. "What do you want with me?"

"I've already told you."

"Who are you?"

"Not a bad question. I'm the Bargainer. I make deals for people; in this case for Underboss."

"Who's this Underboss?"

"Doesn't matter yet. Besides, if I told you, you might not want to deal with him or me. Let's focus on what's important here. So, Ronan, do you want your daughter back alive or not?"

Ronan sat there pondering what he was hearing. He turned from looking at the huge man, placed his head on the steering wheel and thought: *The dead only come back to life in the movies . . .*

"I'll leave you to decide, friend," the Bargainer said in a kindly voice. "I'll walk up to the barn and wait for you there. I know this is hard for you, so take your time. Just remember, your truck will only run in reverse."

Ronan didn't reply. He had no idea what to say and so said nothing. He heard the sound of the man walking off. He remained there with his forehead on the steering wheel, while the sky darkened above him, and tried to convince himself that the man he'd just spoken to was merely playing a sick joke on him.

But the conviction in the tall man's words nagged at him. The 'Bargainer,' as he'd called himself, had spoken like he meant what he said. As if he *could* actually reverse Cathy's death.

Ronan figured it was worth a try. *He wants me to do something for him in exchange? What can he possibly want that will outweigh bringing Cathy back to me?*

Ronan was a bereaved parent. And any parent worth their salt would give their right arm or leg to bring their child back to life again.

No, Ronan thought fiercely. *Not just an arm or a leg. I'll give everything I own in this damn world to have my baby girl back alive again. I'll even sell my soul to the Devil himself.*

Once convinced that he was about doing the right thing, Ronan started up the truck again.

The Bargainer hadn't been lying. The pickup truck *would* only run in reverse. So, with impatience mounting in him, Ronan Higgins reversed the white vehicle all the way back to his farm.

Ronan sped the vehicle backward as fast as he could. Still, he couldn't catch up with the thin, oversized figure reflected in the rearview mirror. The Bargainer slowly widened the distance between himself and the following pickup truck.

After a while, Ronan noticed too that the sky over his farm seemed oddly darker than was usual for this time of evening, almost as if the giant's black clothes were staining the sky.

He gulped and kept reversing. He had the sudden impression that his recent thought about selling his soul to the Devil might not be too far off the mark after all.

But he'd meant it: he'd do literally anything to bring Cathy back again.

***

By the time Ronan parked beside the farmhouse, he could see the tall man striding away between the sunflowers towards the distant barn where Cathy had died.

Ronan watched him go. He tried to estimate the man's height from his strides. All he could tell was that the fellow was unnaturally tall. Ronan felt a sudden suspicion—that the Bargainer had been the one who'd killed Cathy. But that couldn't be; because if the man had done so, how come then that Ronan had met him walking *towards* the farm while he'd been driving out? From their meeting point, the barn where Cathy died lay almost a mile in the opposite direction.

The Bargainer had by now reached the far-off barn. Ronan watched him duck through the entrance.

No, not unnaturally tall . . . he's supernaturally tall, Ronan corrected himself, setting out after the man.

And no, he'd not just been imagining it: an unnatural gloom did now hang over his farm. Ronan couldn't explain it, but now even his glorious sunflower fields seemed spooky.

CHAPTER 3

Ronan & the Bargainer

When Ronan reached the barn, the Bargainer already had Cathy up off the floor and lying on the large workbench at the back of the building. Ronan was relieved that he'd not been there to witness the man pulling Cathy's head off the pickaxe spike. He couldn't have stood the sight without puking.

He strode over and joined the Bargainer by the workbench. Now that they were side by side, he finally got a proper estimate of the man's height.

At the very least, he's got to be eight feet tall. Ronan, who was six foot tall himself, barely reached the Bargainer's chest.

"Alright, what now?" Ronan asked. Staring at the dead teenager laid out on the long wooden table, he questioned his expectations. Even to himself they seemed crazy. *She's dead, you fool, and the dead don't come back! How dare you expect anything else. Just look at that huge hole in her head! You can see her brains in there. You're expecting this weird stranger to perform a miracle. Miracles don't happen anymore.*

Only, Ronan was very certain this wouldn't be a *divine* miracle. Now that he was more composed, Ronan sensed a 'badness' radiating from his companion. If holiness existed as a measureable quantity, then this tall fellow standing next to him had nothing to do with it. He was anti-holy. He exuded evil like body odor.

Still, if God wouldn't raise Cathy, maybe the Devil would.

Ronan grimaced at the sight of the girl. She was all bloody about the head and shoulders. Her one dangling and one staring eye made her look really grotesque.

The Bargainer now began stripping Cathy naked. Ronan restrained his paternal need to protest. In silence he watched the tall man peel off his daughter's brown work shirt, her sneakers and her denim pants;

the clothes splattered with gore and with muck from the barn floor. His companion dumped the clothes to one side and dropped the dead girl's underwear on top of them.

"Okay, time to do it," he whispered, speaking more to himself than to Ronan. He pulled out a large jar from his black jacket and spilled a pale blue jelly into his left palm. It was a large pile of goop. Ronan estimated that the Bargainer's hands were each large enough to completely engulf a human head.

"Help me spread her legs."

Ronan balked for a moment. It was bad enough seeing Cathy naked.

"Spread her legs wide and hold them apart. I gotta get some of this jelly inside her."

Ronan parted Cathy's legs and folded them back up against her chest. He shut his eyes when the tall man began scooping the jelly from his palm and shoving it inside Cathy's vagina. The slurping sounds the man's huge fingers made almost made Ronan sick. The jelly also stank.

"She wasn't a virgin then," the Bargainer said. "Not that it really matters."

There were some more slurping noises, then the man told Ronan, "Alright, you can let her go now."

Ronan opened his eyes. He lowered Cathy's legs back onto the table. Her thighs now had a light-blue sheen to them.

"Time to do her head." The Bargainer scooped the blue jelly into the hole in Cathy's face. He packed it in deep with a finger, until it dripped out of the larger hole in the back of her head.

"Okay, that's about enough." Like one stoppering up a bottle, the Bargainer pushed Cathy's displaced right eye back into its socket. This plugged up most of the wound in her face. He plugged the rear wound with her hair.

The Bargainer smeared the remaining jelly in his hand over Cathy's face, then whispered a spell over her:

"L'ri gelt tilpue sir,
Dool b foda ets nisni evru oy'h'gu orht won wolf livetel,
Efil fodaetsni s'b milru o yevom h'taeddna,
E fiwsi here wu oyhguo ht sakrow sliv edeh two n'mrofrep."

There was a miniature thunderclap inside the barn. The next moment, to Ronan's shock, Cathy sat up. She still had that bloody crack on the right side of her face where the eye socket had fractured, but her blue eyes focused on her father with recognition.

"Damn, dad, have I got one hell of a headache," she said. Then her eyes went blank and she slumped back down again, smacking her head on the workbench.

An immense chill ran through Ronan. He stared up at the Bargainer, a pleading look in his eyes.

"Please . . ." he stuttered. He couldn't put the rest of it in words. Seeing Cathy revive just now had felt as if he was the one waking up from the dead. And seeing her flop back down had felt like he was dying with her. "Please," he groaned. "Whatever you want . . ."

The Bargainer had a smile on his face. "She'll be okay now. The first burst of revival always happens like that." He pointed at the girl. "Look at her chest."

Ronan looked. Cathy's chest was rising and falling as if she was breathing. He looked back up at the tall man.

The Bargainer nodded down at him. "What's happening now is that the jelly's replacing her brain cells. The process will take a while to complete." He gestured a huge finger at Ronan. "In the meantime, you and I need to have a little chat."

Ronan nodded nervously. "Sure, whatever you say."

"Come with me."

Ronan followed the Bargainer out of the barn. They stood there by the barn entrance, the man of normal height and the overly-tall man, facing west. The nearby Massachusetts mountains had the outline of orange sunset to them.

"So what do you want me to do?" Ronan asked, his delight at Cathy's miraculous revival now tempered by the knowledge that payment for the miracle was required.

The Bargainer pulled a small leather pouch from one of his pockets. He loosened its string, then spilled its contents into his palm. He held out his hand for Ronan to see. His palm contained a pile of little spheres, each of them a color swirl of red, green, and blue marbled on black. Each of them was also visibly pulsing, throbbing as if alive.

"What are these?" Ronan enquired with some misgiving.

The Bargainer laughed. "They're seeds, man. You're a farmer, Ronan. I just need you to plant them for me."

Ronan didn't even want to touch the hellish-looking 'seeds.' But still . . . "Plant them where?" he asked. "Among my sunflowers? Or out back, with the corn?"

The Bargainer jerked a thumb at the barn behind them. "In there. You aren't using it at the moment."

Ronan figured that wouldn't be too much trouble. "Alright," he agreed.

The Bargainer put the seeds away in their leather pouch and passed them to Ronan. Even within the pouch, they had a horrible feel to them. They throbbed like beating hearts and were noticeably hot. And like the Bargainer, they had an inexplicable sense of 'badness' to them.

"How long do they take to grow?" Ronan asked.

"Not long: two to three days at most, depending on the quality of the fertilizer. Then I'll harvest them and be on my way."

"Alright."

"It won't be as easy as you think, though. There are special conditions attached to these seeds . . . but remember what you get in return—your daughter alive and well."

"I'm listening, man. So long as Cathy remains alive and well, I'll do anything you want."

"She will."

"Are you assuring me of that?"

"Yeah, I am."

"Okay."

"Good. We understand ourselves well. Now listen . . ."

Ronan listened. The more he heard, the more appalled he grew. No, he couldn't do *this*. This was just monstrous. It was insane.

But, he pondered, wasn't bringing a dead girl back to life insane too?

So, Ronan listened some more. A whole lot more, while the Bargainer explained what he was expected to do. He'd have some assistance 'from below,' the gaunt giant promised, but the responsibility for producing the crop from the seeds would rest on him.

And no, there wasn't any danger, the Bargainer assured him . . . Hell looked after its own.

CHAPTER 4

Ronan

At first Ronan thought he'd never be able to go through with it. What was being demanded from him was much too horrible to seriously consider doing.

But then Cathy called him from inside the barn—"Hey, dad? Where the hell are you? And why are all my clothes on the floor? Were you fiddling with me in my sleep?"—and amidst the surge of joy he felt at just hearing her voice, he resolved that he had to keep her alive.

Yes, he was going to keep his darling daughter alive, whatever it took.

He smiled up at the Bargainer. It was a crooked and horrible smile, the smile of a man who realizes he's just sold his soul to the Devil, but doesn't care. "Man, you got yourself a deal," he said, shaking the pouch of throbbing seeds. "You can count on me to get the job done."

This statement instantly shifted Ronan Higgins from the grade of 'sane' to 'not exactly sane anymore.' It was a subtle mental alteration, one which Ronan himself never noticed. But with his promise to the Bargainer, this previously nice and caring man had moved over into an infernal darkness; into realms of evil experience he'd never previously imagined existed.

From his companion's words, Ronan suspected he was going to see some really strange things—he just had no idea how strange.

What he did know, however, was that he was suddenly filled with an exciting anticipation to get to work. It was as though the seeds he needed to plant were taking him over and urging him to get started on the task of growing them.

Then he remembered something and scowled up at the Bargainer. "Hey, dude, now that we're on the same page, get your damn warlock hex off my truck, wilya? I *still* need to drive into town." He gestured toward the two nearby cellphone towers. "The phones ain't working and if I'm to do what you want, I need to get ahold of my niece Sylvia to confirm that yes, her party's still on."

The Bargainer's not-quite-Mexican face creased in a cold smile. (Now Ronan was struck by the thought that the tall man resembled a certain dead country music singer, but he couldn't remember exactly which one. No, it wasn't Merle Haggard or George Jones, nor Jim Reeves. But he looked like someone famous, for sure.)

"Oh, I'm the one who turned all your telecommunications off," the Bargainer said. "No one can either call in or out from the farm. Gimme a minute to fix it."

For a few seconds his eyes went completely black, as black as if chunks of coal had been shoved into their sockets.

When the Bargainer's eyes reverted back to normal again, he said, "Done. You can use your phones now. Your truck will run forward too."

Ronan pulled out his cellphone. Yes, it seemed to be working fine now.

Cathy appeared at the barn door then. Apart from the blood in her hair and on her face, she was her normal self again.

She was struck speechless by the Bargainer's height. She was a tall young woman but barely reached his waist.

She stood there, her mouth agape, staring at him.

"It's alright, girl," he said with a smile. "No need to be frightened of me. I'm a good friend of your father's." He looked west, at the sunset. "In fact, I was just about leaving." He nodded down at Ronan. "I may drop by during the week for a beer or two. Keep some Bud Light on hand." Then he winked. "Next weekend, then? So I can make arrangements with Underboss for backup."

Ronan nodded. "Yeah, next weekend for sure. It's a birthday party, so there's no chance of it being cancelled even for bad weather. We'll just put a tent up for everyone or hold the party inside the farmhouse."

The Bargainer nodded. He lifted his hat to Cathy, "See you around, young woman," then strode off left across the sunflower fields.

Cathy stared after him for a while, saying, "Dad, I didn't think God made people that tall. And where's he going anyway? The highway is the other way."

"Huh?"

She turned to look at her father. His cellphone was ringing and his attention was on it. "Your friend," she explained, pointing north. "Where's he head—"

She'd turned back and the Bargainer had vanished. All that stretched ahead of her were acres of sunflower blossoms, with the pond visible on her right where the land dipped.

Cathy turned back to her father. "Dad? Did you see . . . ?"

"How's your head, darling?" he asked to distract her. He had the phone pressed to his ear and was listening.

"Fine, the headache's gone. But I had a nightmare where I was in this really hot place and . . ."

"Shush. Your cousin's on the line. . . . Hi, Sylvia. . . . Yeah, we're still on. . . . You've been calling me for two hours? . . . Dammit. I dunno what's wrong with all these mobile carriers nowadays. . . . Sure, we're ready for next weekend. . . ."

CHAPTER 5

Cathy

While her father finalized the preparations for her cousin's birthday party, Cathy tried to recall what had happened to her.

She couldn't remember much, except that she'd gone to the barn to fetch the chainsaw for her father and then . . . and then . . . after that everything was blank until she'd woken up naked on the workbench with that bluish jelly on her thighs and blood on her head and shoulders.

It's crazy. When I opened my eyes that first time, I felt like I'd died and revived again.

She felt inexplicably odd, like she was a different person from before. Before? Why would she even imagine a 'before?' She'd simply walked over to the barn and then . . . her life had altered in some drastic way.

She waited for her father to get off the phone. Maybe he could fill her in on what had happened to her in the barn.

In the meantime, she wondered how the tall man had suddenly vanished. His disappearance had been as abrupt as if he'd fallen into a hole in the ground.

CHAPTER 6

A Week Later . . . Ben, Snort & Liza

Ben Hiller was in a lot of trouble.

At the moment he was stuck in a hole in the forest floor that reached up over his head. This wasn't accidental. The two people who'd put him in the hole, a drug dealer named Snort and his girlfriend Liza, were smiling down at him.

"How's that feel?" Snort asked. "If you're not comfy yet, you will be once we start shoveling in the sand."

Ben couldn't reply. They'd duct-taped his mouth over so he couldn't scream for help. They'd duct-taped his wrists and ankles together too, so he couldn't climb out of the pit they'd dumped him in. In addition, they'd shot Ben up with some drug that had weakened him so much he was finding it hard to even stay on his feet.

The hole was about six feet deep and three wide. Ben was five-foot-eight. As Snort had explained to Liza while they were rolling Ben into the hole, "it's just deep enough to suffocate him before he's able to climb out."

"But the cops," she'd protested.

"There's no one around."

"What about the music we're hearing over there?"

They'd all heard the music: loud trance, techno, and hip-hop, coming from a quarter-mile away.

"Sounds like one hell of a party," Liza said. "And it's on this same farmland, ain't it?"

"At the farmhouse, but it's a one-off," Snort had replied. "I had a good look around when I came to dig this damn grave. Both times I was here, I never once saw anybody step over this way." He'd paused, then pointed into the darkened tree foliage. "There's an old barn out there somewhere and lots of sunflowers. The farmer and his daughter go out there a lot, but they never venture in this direction."

Once Ben was down in the pit, Snort had lit up a joint. He was in no hurry to fetch the shovels from the trunk of his car. It was barely 10 p.m.—they had lots of time. Literal time to kill. Snort wanted his victim to appreciate how little life he had left. He wanted Ben to feel his life slipping away between his fingers, like water filtering through a basket, with himself powerless to halt the drainage.

He'd passed the joint to Liza, explaining further: "So, this place is perfect. Once I cover the son-of-a-bitch up, I'll heap additional sand over it, then conceal it further with all that brush over there. With all these trees everywhere, it'll be fifty years before anyone finds him, if they ever do."

Liza had puffed and nodded.

Ben thought Snort was getting high to fill himself with the necessary courage to commit murder.

This was no consolation to Ben. This pot-pause was the tranquility before the tempest. This looked like curtains for Ben. The end of the road for certain. He saw no chance of his being rescued. Just two shovels and some sweating stood between himself and death.

"Hey, can you feel the worms wriggling yet?" Liza asked. She was referring to the fact that they'd stripped Ben naked before dropping him in there. Snort wanted his brand-new jeans and jacket. "Once we fill the hole in, the nightcrawlers are gonna tunnel into you, man. They're gonna eat you alive. You're gonna be praying to die quick. For real."

Pothead logic, like she bypassed high school biology. Ben squinted up at Liza. It was too dark to really see her face. They were out somewhere in the west Massachusetts woods with heavy tree cover blocking out the moon. The only light here came from the flashlight app on Snort's phone. Still, he made out Liza's eyes. Pale in the daytime, tonight they were dark pools in her pale face, gleaming with excitement. She was jacked up on narcotics, high too on what she and Snort were doing to him. Impatient to get things over with, she passed the time shaking her ass to the distant music.

"One great thing about raving in the countryside," she told Snort, "there's no neighbors to piss off, or to piss *you* off, for that matter. Hey, baby, once we get through burying Ben, let's crash that party over there. Maybe they can use some of your product."

Snort nodded. "Now there's a plan. I got some coke and MDMA in the trunk that I need to move quick."

Ben switched his gaze over to Snort. The short crew-cut fellow was finishing off the joint. He was called Snort because he loved cocaine.

Dope, dope, dope.

I'm a dope for doing dope, Ben thought grimly. *Mom always warned me. I never listened and now look where it's gotten me.*

Ben had been smoking pot when they'd come for him. He'd been too stoned to mount any resistance. (Even now, with his life dangling by a thread, he was still stoned.) And to keep him docile, Snort had injected him with that something that made his limbs feel like waterlogged logs floating down the Mississippi River.

CHAPTER 7

Ben – The Toilet

Dope. Drugs.

Ben Hiller was a smalltime Springfield crook. 25, good-looking, blonde hair. He dealt drugs, mostly pot and cocaine.

Ben's current problem stemmed from a tragicomedy of errors:

A week ago, at about 1 a.m. in the morning, he'd woken up to a loud banging on his apartment door and shouts of, "Hey—Open this goddamn door right now, Hiller, you hear me—it's da police! We know you're dealing drugs in there, Hiller! You're going away forever this time!"

Believing the cops to be about raiding his dingy apartment, Ben had flushed the quarter kilo of cocaine Snort had left with him down the toilet. He'd trashed the package paper, then opened the door to let the police in.

Only it hadn't been the police at Ben's door. It had been Snort and Liza and Monkey, a friend of theirs, pranking him. Monkey had been the one who'd done the cop voice, so Ben wouldn't recognize who was shouting.

Ben was flabbergasted. "What'd you pull a nutjob stunt like that for, man? I just flushed your coke down the shitter."

Snort, of course, didn't believe this. He thought Ben had sold the drugs and pocketed the money. All Ben's explanations had fallen on deaf ears. As had his pleading that he'd pay the money back soonest.

Hence Ben's current predicament. This idiot called Snort was about killing him over a problem he'd caused himself. But then there was Snort for you—all nose and no brains.

CHAPTER 8

Ben, Snort & Lisa, Pt.2

When Snort finished his joint, he grabbed hold of Liza, who was still dancing to the distant music.

"Hey, what you want, man?"

"I want you. Take your pants off."

"What? Here? Now? Why?"

"Why not? I got a massive hard-on. Here, feel it."

"Wow, baby, it's really hard. Like steel. Like Superman's cock! Superdick! But . . . but . . . shouldn't we kill him first? Let's fetch the shovels from the car and . . ."

"Liza, honey, just slip the damn pants off."

"Er . . . em . . ." Being quite high herself, Liza couldn't think of a suitable reason not to have sex beside the man they intended burying alive. Snort peeled her pants off, pushed her down on her hands and knees, and slipped his penis inside her.

"Hey, Ben, you're a movie star!" he laughed. "This flick we're shooting is called 'I Fuck On Your Grave!'"

Liza began getting into it, the thrill of the kill making her horny. She moaned as Snort thrust into her.

The pair were right by the pit's edge. Ben could see the glow in her eyes, her pale thin face reflected in phone light. Her lips distorted with passion. Her face shiny with cold sweat. Her brown hair moving like wind-ruffled drapes.

Behind her, a smirk on his ugly face, Snort looked desperate to ejaculate. He was grunting like a happy farm hog.

The noise of their bodies coming together. The slurp of penis in vagina. Liza's fingers digging deep into the earth as she neared orgasm. More gasps and moans.

"Hey, Ben, I spy you getting a boner down there from ogling my tits," Liza gasped. "Wow, baby, he's about to come. He's not just a thief, he's a sleazy perv too!"

This was a lie. Ben's penis was so limp, it could easily be mistaken for one of the nightcrawlers that Liza expected to soon start tunneling through him. Sex was so far from his mind, it might have ridden a Greyhound bus down to Florida.

Still, Snort and Liza had a good laugh over that.

Liza giggled down at him. Her body jerked back and forth with each penile invasion. "Oh, boy, you gotta be hard as hell down there; too bad you can't make love to the dirt."

"Try it!" she moaned a second later. "Stick your boner deep in the side of the hole and see if you can't get Mother Earth preggered up."

"Yeah," Snort laughed, "someone has to! How else are the trees gonna grow?"

Ben wanted to climb out and wring Snort's neck. Then he'd dump Liza in the hole and fill it in. But he felt as weak and uncoordinated as a newborn baby. The only reason he was fighting to stay on his feet was so he didn't make it easier for them to kill him. He knew that if he dared sit down in the pit, he'd never manage to stand up again. And then a mere covering of four feet of earth might suffice to suffocate him.

Finally his captors were done having sex. Ben was by now covered in spittle that Liza had drooled on him during her orgasm.

Liza got up and pulled her pants up. Snort buckled his belt, then retrieved his cellphone from where it lay on the grass.

"Any signal yet?" Liza asked.

Snort shook his head. "None whatsoever." He peeked down into the hole. "Hey, Ben, don't go anywhere. We'll be back in a bit to finish what *you* started."

"We just gotta fetch the shovels," Liza added. "Won't be more than a few minutes."

Snort picked up Ben's bundled clothes. "Yeah, asshole, sufficient time to say your last prayers. Or to convert to a new religion if you feel the sudden urge."

With that, the pair of them sauntered off arm-in-arm, with Snort telling Liza, "That son-of-a-bitch must be worse than crazy if he ever imagined I was gonna buy that bullshit story of him flushing my snow down the toilet. When he gets down to Hell even the Devil ain't gonna believe anyone could be so stupid as to mess with me like that."

"Yeah. You're really showing him, baby."

And then they were gone. Ben was left with just the darkness to keep him company. And a countdown to eternity in his mind. And the sound of the distant party.

Sounded like someone's birthday.

Life was really ironic, wasn't it? Here he was about to die because of someone else's mistake, while less than a mile away, a bunch of people were living it up.

It was right at that moment that the music stopped playing.

Taking into account the distance, the noise of the forest at night, and all the drugs in his system, Ben wasn't sure what he heard after that, but some of it sounded like loud screaming.

CHAPTER 9

Party People

"Let's take a break, baby," Sylvia Stewart shouted so as to be heard over the music. "I need to use the ladies."

Her boyfriend Barry McCain nodded. They slipped away from the dancing throng.

"Don't take too long," Barry said and then walked over to lean against his car.

Plastic cup of beer in hand, Sylvia headed for the farmhouse.

Partly to let her uncle Ronan get some sleep tonight, partly because the recent rains had muddied up the farmhouse yard and rendered it unsuitable for dancing, but mostly because this was where they'd found the best location to set up the DJ stage, the party was occurring a hundred yards out from the farmhouse, on the eastern edge of the sunflower fields.

The company contracted to put up the stage had also put down a makeshift floor for the partiers so their furniture and feet wouldn't get bogged down in the damp earth.

The DJ's stage was twenty feet wide, raised three feet off the ground, and bordered on each side by two stacks of massive speakers. Tricolored stage lights lit up both DJ and dancers. The music was loud enough that the partiers felt its vibrations as a physical sensation. The hip-hop tracks in particular felt like someone had packaged portable earthquakes for entertainment.

The party was bouncing. That could be taken literally. At the moment celebrity DJ Amy Fox was spinning *Bounce* by the Non-Repressed Girls. The track had a beat that made everyone hop like a bunny.

Amy Fox—pale, skinny, platinum blonde, blue lipstick; white pantsuit and white boots—was really rocking the party.

Pausing in her flight to the toilet, Sylvia caught Amy's eye. She gave the DJ a thumbs up, then blew her a happy kiss and waved. Amy waved back, dancing while doing so. Then, returning her attention to her turntables and putting her headphones on, she began mixing the Non-Repressed Girls into the latest Katie Perry single. The dancers sent up a loud cheer as Katie's voice came up on the speakers. Everyone began shaking with renewed energy.

The moon was out, the clouds were out and there was a slight wind. Sylvia basked in the moonlight. She had weather report assurance that it wouldn't rain tonight.

Sylvia sipped her drink. She was delighted with how her birthday party was going. It was a roaring success. Exactly how she and Barry had planned it. Thirty friends of hers having a good time over Saturday and Sunday. (Because she was thirty today, she thought the number symbolic.) To avoid jealousies and boredom they'd mostly asked couples. The five or six singles present were Sylvia's work buddies from Bain & Company.

Lodging would be in the farmhouse. The old building had lots of unused rooms. Since it was just for one night, the singles could sleep downstairs in the living room. They'd shipped in enough mattresses for everyone.

Any of the singles who'd paired up and wanted to make love could do so out in Amy Fox's equipment tent. That though would clearly only work on a 'first come, first served' basis.

Sylvia laughed. 'First come' indeed. 'First coming' in the DJ's tent also depended on if Amy Fox wasn't having her own sexual party in there. Sylvia had noticed the platinum-blonde girl flirting with two of the singles before the party started. Amy reputedly liked sex a lot.

There were quite a few vehicles on the premises. Sylvia and her guests' rides, Amy's SUV, and two trucks belonging to the company (owned by a friend) that had built the stage and provided the sound system. The vehicles were parked rather haphazardly, but there weren't so many of them that their arrangement constituted a problem.

She looked beyond the dancing couples. Her boyfriend was now beside the barbeque grill, chatting over beers with Ron Howard from her office. Or rather, Barry and Ron were trying to hold a conversation. She watched them shouting answers at one another. The loudness of the music precluded any normal conversation.

So far, almost all the invitees had arrived. Two couples weren't yet here though: the Donnellys and the Warrens. She expected both to arrive before midnight.

And then it would be party time. Well, actually it was already party time. It would just be more party time then.

She checked her watch. 10 p.m.

Katie Perry finished singing. The next song was *Rich Bitch,* an Aerosmith/Run DMC-style collaboration by Slain Jane and hip hop artist Puff Badder:

"I hate your lipstick, bitch,
But I really wish it worked.
I wish it glued your lips together,
Once and for all.

Your eyebrows look so sharp,
They got that razor arc.
I hope they slice into your empty skull,
And let the airhead gas out . . ."

Giggling at the lyric, Sylvia now remembered why she'd left Barry's side. *I need to pee.* She hurried over to the farmhouse.

As Sylvia stepped up onto the farm building's front porch, she pondered an oddity. Since their arrival here at her uncle's farm, everyone's cellphones had stopped working. Same went for tablets and laptop modems. Even the farmhouse phone wasn't working.

We're all completely cut off from the outside world here.

Uncle Ronan said the lack of cell coverage had started a week ago, and phone reception had been switching on and off intermittently since then. It *was* possible to call from the state highway, where phone signals abruptly returned, but that was a 5-minute drive away. No one was about driving five minutes just to make a phone call, except it was an emergency.

Let's hope we don't have any emergencies then. As added assurance, while stepping through the front door she made sure to touch the wooden door frame.

CHAPTER 10

Sylvia

While crossing the living room, Sylvia noticed her cousin Cathy descending the stairway.

On seeing the girl, Sylvia lost her desire to pee. Cathy was wearing a short sleeveless white dress and black boots. But it was her face that gave Sylvia the shivers. She'd painted it white as a mask, with jet-black lips and eyelids. Her blond hair was done up in two long braids that dangled down her back.

Why the hell would she make herself up like this for a birthday party?

Cathy descended the stairs slowly, trailing her hand along the bannister as if she was sleepwalking. She stared dreamily ahead of her.

"Hi, cousin," Sylvia said, getting a handle on the fear she felt rising in her belly. "You do know Halloween's still a month off, yeah?"

"Die, baby," Cathy replied with a soporific smile. At least that's what it sounded like she'd said.

"Huh?"

Cathy giggled. "I said 'diet.' I've been thinking I need to go on a diet soonest. On a farm there's nothing to do except get fat."

"Oh, that's what you said." Sylvia regarded the girl. She didn't think Cathy had said 'diet.' And why would Cathy diet anyway? She only weighed about 140 pounds. She was tall too, so the weight was evenly distributed on her. This was in sharp contrast to Sylvia, who was short, dark, and bordering on fleshy (and who nonetheless didn't feel the slightest urge to lose weight). Except Cathy had suddenly gotten anorexic. But could farmer's daughters suffer from eating disorders with all that healthy food everywhere?

"So how does it feel to be so old?" Cathy asked. "I mean, thirty must be . . ."

"You'll know when you get there," Sylvia replied. "Eleven years isn't too long a wait."

Cathy shrugged. "Yeah, I guess you're right. But it seems so far off. Like old age, you know." She spoke like she was stoned. "Hey, 'fore I forget to mention it—dad says to tell everyone to have fun and not worry about the noise bothering him. He's busy in the huge barn out back."

Sylvia nodded. She'd not seen her uncle since the party started. "What's with the gothic makeup anyway? You look like you just stepped out of Elvira's tomb."

"Oh, nothing. I just feel creepy tonight. Ghoulish. The moon's bringing out the darkness in me."

"Well, hold it in check when you join the party. Keep your evil self caged. Don't scare my guests."

The broad black grin on the girl's whitewashed face filled Sylvia with an instant urge to pee again. It wasn't just the ghoulish makeup either. Something about Cathy now struck Sylvia as very odd. Cathy seemed not-quite-herself. She'd always been a bit of a dreamy girl, but now she seemed like someone from another planet.

She looks possessed, Sylvia thought with a shudder. *Like Goth overload studying to be a witch.*

Outside, the music changed. Pop-rock guitars and a sultry tenor voice over a dance beat.

"Great music," Cathy said, bobbing her head to it.

"I'll see you outside," Sylvia said, then hurried off to the toilet.

Behind her, Cathy peeked out of the front door and then walked quickly back through the house into the kitchen. There she stood in front of the row of racked knives, trying to make up her mind which of them she preferred for the night's business.

Finally, a black smile on her face, she selected two long carving knives.

CHAPTER 11

Barry

Sylvia's boyfriend Barry McCain was sipping wine when the lights went off. The music died and everyone was left in the darkness.

Amidst the chorus of disappointed groans as the dancers returned to their seats, Barry got up, flicked on a flashlight, and went to see what was wrong.

They'd powered the lights and equipment by running a long cable from the first of the three barns behind the farmhouse out into the field. The light was still on in the barn. So, it looked like someone had either unplugged the cable, or they'd switched the socket off. Or the fuse had blown from overload. Barry dismissed this third possibility: the barn in question housed several large food processing machines, each of which surely had to use more power than twelve light bulbs and an amplifier system.

Two friends, Mark and Tony, jogged after Barry. Together the three men made their way across to the barn.

The cable was still plugged in and the power was still on. Mark, the electrician who'd laid the power cable, checked out the barn's fuse box. Everything was fine there too.

"Only one thing for it," he told Barry. "Something's cracked the cable."

"How's that even possible?" Barry didn't see how anything could crack this power cable. The damn thing was two inches thick.

"It can happen," Mark assured him. "Freak conditions, for sure. We just need to locate the break and repair it. I've got tools in the truck. Shouldn't take too long to fix—maybe twenty minutes or so."

They stepped out into the night again and began tracing the cable back to the party. For aesthetics sake, Mark had run the power line through the border of the sunflower fields. That way no one could trip over it while drunk either.

Mark walked in the lead with his flashlight trained on the ground. Barry was in the middle. Tony brought up the rear.

"Hey, you guys, I can see eyes among the plants," Tony said suddenly. "Red eyes."

Barry turned back towards the dark thickset man. Tony was already tipsy and seemed rather unsteady on his feet.

"Dude, you're drunk," Barry said.

"Guys, I'm serious." Tony swung his flashlight beam through the sunflower rows. The beam seemed to alight on something. "What are those things?"

Barry looked but couldn't tell. To see better, he aimed his own flashlight in the same direction. Okay, now there did seem to be shadows moving through the sunflowers. About thirty yards off. Shadows that weren't a natural part of the night.

Feeling suddenly uneasy, he turned quickly back towards Mark. But Mark was now twenty yards ahead of them, his eyes to the ground as he tracked down the cable break.

Barry looked back along Tony's flashlight beam. There was nothing to see anymore. He thought he heard the sound of rustling leaves moving away from them, towards the party. And there was also a weird smell of burning which he couldn't attribute to the barbeques. It smelt like leaves on fire.

"They've vanished," Tony said. "I don't like this, man. I mean it— those things did have red eyes. Like a pack of wolves standing up on their hind legs."

"Werewolves? You're kidding me, right?" But he saw that Tony wasn't joking. Tony didn't look tipsy anymore. Instead, his face was lined with worry.

Barry gulped; suddenly he didn't like this. He felt vulnerable, being outside on a farm with midnight approaching and with the power gone. And with no way to summon help if they ran into trouble.

He tugged Tony's sleeve. "Come on, let's catch up with Mark. The sooner we get the power restored, the better for our nerves. Or else we're all gonna start seeing things."

"I'm *not* seeing things."

"Whatever, dude. Just come on."

They turned towards Mark, who'd stopped ten yards ahead and was bent over the cable. Twenty yards beyond the electrician, the birthday celebrations were continuing in the glow of battery-powered lamps. Someone was telling a joke. People were laughing.

Barry wondered if Sylvia was back from using the bathroom yet. He grinned. That was one amusing thing about women and the great outdoors: if she'd been a guy she could simply have stepped behind one of the trucks to handle her bathroom business; but, no, she'd been worried about a farm bug crawling up her legs or biting her buttocks while she squatted.

He thought of calling her, then scowled. This damn farm! No one's phone had gotten even a single signal bar since they'd arrived here.

"Have you found it?" he asked Mark.

Mark stared up at him, a perplexed look on his face. "Yeah. But this don't make any sense. See for yourself." He moved back so Barry could see and shone his light on the break.

Even without being told, Barry could see what had Mark so confused. The power cable hadn't just been broken through, it had melted. And not in just one place either. Over a length of half a yard, there were four similar four-inch gaps in the cable. In each instance both the thick electric wires and their plastic sheaths had been liquefied.

"How?" Barry began, recalling the weird smell of burning that had come wafting through the sunflower field. And now too, something seemed very wrong. He felt a deep unease that he couldn't explain.

"Man, I dunno how this is even possible . . ." Mark began saying, then a quizzical look came over his features. "Hey, where's Tony?"

Barry looked back. Tony had vanished. "He's probably tripped over his feet and fallen into the sunflowers . . . I'll go find him." The burning smell was back again. And much denser now. This time it smelt like roasting meat. But . . . the barbeque was on the other side of the dance floor.

Mark scratched his head. "Yeah, you do that. I'll fetch the tools and some terminal blocks and also get some guys to help pull the cable together again."

Barry started back the way they'd come. He took three steps and suddenly all hell broke out around him.

First, everybody over at the party began screaming at once. Next, he heard Tony yell, "Help, they've got me!" followed by a horrible snapping sound like someone was breaking wood, and then . . .

He spun towards Mark and froze. Something was standing over Mark. It was about man-sized, but Barry didn't really see it clearly. Some intuitive sense of self-preservation had made him instantly switch off his torch. So all he saw was a shadow, but a shadow that seemed to be burning. Its body was filled with glowing crevices.

He stood there watching. Mark hadn't yet noticed the shadow thing. He was just about straightening up. How Mark hadn't noticed the thing was a mystery to Barry. Because the damn thing *reeked*. It didn't smell so much like barbeque, but like a barbeque grill did in-between changing steaks, sizzling from all the meat juice that had dripped on it, both present and past; that smell of roasted air which alerted one to the presence and danger of intense heat.

Indeed, now that Barry thought on it, the shadowy thing reminded him of glowing coals.

"Mark!" he whispered harshly. "Mark!"

Mark turned around then and gasped. He was still bringing up his flashlight to look at what was behind him, when the thing stuck its fingers into his eyes. There was a flash of light. Mark's eyes exploded and steam spurted up from them. Mark began screaming. Next, the dark creature dug burning fingers into Mark's neck. His screams died to a horrible gurgle. Blood squirted from his punctured throat, but instantly boiled and cooked, throwing up white clouds of steam. With Mark's flesh blistering around its hand, the shadowy monster dragged the blinded man off into the sunflowers.

Barry sensed motion behind him. He spun around, saw another shadow reaching flaming fingers for him. Just like Tony had said, this one had glowing red eyes. It seemed to be a man, but a man made of burning coal.

Barry ducked out of reach of its outstretched hands, then turned and sprinted off in the only direction that seemed safe, back towards the farmhouse.

As he ran, he hoped Sylvia hadn't yet left the farmhouse.

Behind him the screaming continued unabated.

CHAPTER 12

Sylvia

Sylvia was still in the farmhouse

She'd reached the toilet in a subdued state of mind. Cathy's creepy makeup had depressed her. *This is my birthday, not some ghoul's funeral.*

Sylvia had also had a sense of something spooky building up, an inexplicable evil tension in the atmosphere.

She was about to step inside the toilet, when noises spilled out through the ajar door. She peeped. The sight that met her eyes caused her to fling a hand over her mouth to stifle a shocked exclamation.

One of the couples—the Lorens—were having sex in the toilet.

Sylvia chuckled at the sight. It was a welcome change from meeting her creepy cousin.

Sean Loren had Ronnie bent over the washstand, her cream blouse open and her breasts spilling out. Her leather skirt was packed up over her buttocks. Her stockinged legs wobbled in her high heels. Ronnie was grimacing with pleasure and biting her lip as Sean thrust into her from behind.

Amused and a little aroused now, Sylvia slipped quietly away, back to the living room stairs. *I'd best use the bathroom upstairs.*

It was while she was coming downstairs again after peeing that the screaming began.

What the . . . ?

CHAPTER 13

Barry

Barry safely reached the edge of the sunflower plain. He paused there panting. He'd lost his flashlight, but that didn't matter. He was just twenty yards from the farmhouse. Twenty yards from safety. The farm building was on his left, the three barns on his right.

Barry curbed his desire to hurry to the farm building. Yes, his girlfriend Sylvia was in there and he had to make sure she was safe, but now the crazy pandemonium from the party was spreading this way as well.

On his left, less than fifteen yards from where he was concealed, Barry could see two of the same sort of creatures that had taken Mark now grabbing hold of a screaming woman. He squinted; that seemed to be Ronnie Loren. The only illumination here came from the farm buildings and from the moon, which now seemed like a spooky lamp hung from the world's dark ceiling.

Of Ronnie's husband Sean, he saw no sign.

He could make out the 'shadows' more clearly now. In reality they were solid creatures. They looked like black men—paint black, not negro black. Naked and hairless. Neither one had any facial features other than two large red eyes—eyes that were really pits of flame. Their bodies had the texture of roughly sculpted rock. Bright orange gleamed through cracks in their torsos and slits in their limbs, as if their guts and muscles were on fire. Occasionally, as he'd already witnessed, their hands did burst into flame.

It's like they're furnaces, he thought. *Living, walking furnaces.*

Whatever they were, wherever they'd come from (and Barry had no theories about either), the creatures were hot, that was the main thing.

Barry remained where he was. He was terrified. It was already too late to help Ronnie. As with Mark, the first thing the creatures had done to Ronnie Loren was to blind her, digging their fingers into her eyes and boiling them to ash. Next, one of the creatures stuck both of its hands into her chest. Ronnie shrieked at the ghastly insertion. There was a muffled explosion as her heart blew up and exited her corpse in a red gush of mangled meat.

Barry almost wet himself at the horrible sight.

Ronnie Loren slumped to the grass. One of the black creatures began dragging her away by the ankle, walking towards Barry along the dirt track that led between the sunflower fields and the barns. The other creature headed across the farmhouse yard to cut off a fleeing couple.

The creature hauling away Ronnie's corpse passed right in front of Barry. Close enough for him to touch it. It was however intent on its task and didn't see him.

What the hell is this thing?

As it went by, he confirmed his first impression of its appearance. It had neither mouth nor nose nor ears nor hair. Its only facial features were its two eyes. Eyes that glowed demonic orange.

His heart in his mouth, he watched it go, trying not to puke from the dead woman's cooked-meat stink.

Finally, it was gone, vanished away to his right.

The screams and noise had lessened now.

They've killed everyone, Barry thought, in a morbid revelation that filled him with rapidly escalating panic. *Everyone who came here is either dead or dying now. That's why the noise has dropped.*

It was a horrifying thought, imagining himself as the sole survivor of this inexplicable massacre. But still, he hoped Sylvia was alive. So far he'd not heard any screaming coming from the farmhouse. He just had to reach the building.

He readied himself to dash across the clearing. However, there were too many of the hot black creatures in the way. To cut off the partygoers' escape, a line of them had formed in the front farmhouse yard. Proof of the success of this tactic were the five or six mangled and mutilated bodies on the grass near them, two of these without heads. All the corpses smoked as if on fire.

To reach the farmhouse that way would be impossible. He was certain to be seen as he ran across the yard.

So, another tactic was needed. Once the coast was clear enough to attempt flight, Barry ran across to the first barn.

Once safely inside the barn, he tried to shut its door. He then realized he couldn't because of the power cable.

Still, he was hidden in here. He could plan. And from where he was, the monsters wouldn't see him as he attempted to reach the rear farmhouse door. It might be wise to turn off the barn lights though.

Before looking for the light switch, Barry peeked out of the barn entrance. He ducked back in when he saw someone approaching.

A moment later, a woman in a white dress also entered the barn.

"Who . . . ?" Then he realized it was Sylvia's cousin Cathy, done up in heavy Goth makeup, her face all white, her lips black, her eyes rounded by black circles.

"Cathy, where is . . . ?" he began, but then reeled back in pain. He looked down to see what had hurt him. He gaped in surprise. Two large knives were stuck in his belly.

He looked up at the teenager. "What . . . ?"

"Die." Cathy forced both knives deeper into his body. Then, stepping back quickly, she jerked one of them out again and slashed Barry across the neck with it.

Barry's throat opened up wide. Blood gushed fast and thick. He grabbed his neck with both hands. The blood spurted out through his clamped fingers, running down his neck and onto his blue and gold PLUR tee shirt.

Speechless and confused, he stared at Cathy. She was grinning at him and nodding her head.

She looked very crazy.

Giggling, the girl pushed the barn door open. Then she pushed Barry out through it, propelling him forward with a foot on his ass.

Laughing like mad, Cathy ran towards the farmhouse.

Behind her, losing a flood of blood, Barry began counting the seconds to his death.

CHAPTER 14

Sylvia

Scared, Sylvia headed for the rear farmhouse door.

Her single peek out of the front door had convinced her that that wasn't the way to go. She too had seen Ronnie Loren's death.

She'd waited long enough to see Bobby Smith die also. Bobby's head had exploded. One of the black 'men' had grabbed Bobby's head and it had burst to bits like a pumpkin hit with a sledgehammer. On seeing that nastiness, Sylvia had ducked back inside and slammed the front door shut and locked it.

Oh no, I'm not going out there!

The air was a chorus line of screams and moans, agonized whispers and dying groans. Terror and impossible death that made Sylvia wonder if someone had spiked her drink with LSD. This was a hallucination, right?

When earlier she'd stared heavenward, the moon had seemed like a giant zombie eye. In a distressing continuation of her earlier premonition on entering the house, the night now seemed to be raining evil, in invisible psychic droplets that marked all they touched for death.

She had no idea what was going on, why those horrible black things were murdering all her party guests. What were they? Where had they come from? What did they want that could only be appeased by bloodshed?

She suspected, however, that Cathy had something to do with it. The way the little bitch had painted herself up. Like she was attending Death's birthday party, not Sylvia's. The way she'd said "Die" instead of "Hi."

Yes, for sure, Cathy knew what was going on.

Sylvia decided to find the teenager and shake the truth out of her. It was a plan. It was better to be angry than to be scared shitless. Throwing a tantrum was a better reaction that freaking out.

Sylvia did feel enraged. Cathy had ruined her birthday. Yes, the little bitch had. And she had to be held accountable for doing so. And she would be. Sylvia would see to it that she was.

But first, she needed to summon help. Her guests were dying. They needed saving. And she didn't know where Barry was either. Whether he was dead or alive.

She'd already tried the phones, both to call Barry and to summon the cops. The phones were still dead.

Shit!

That left her only one option: to make it to a car and drive down to the main road where all the network signals miraculously picked up again.

Her uncle Ronan's pickup truck was parked by the right of the front porch. She could reach it by sneaking around the rear of the farmhouse. This would also bring her behind the line of monsters that were preventing the guests from fleeing the premises.

So that's what she decided to do.

Sylvia stepped out of the rear door. Almost immediately she saw Cathy coming, approaching from the direction of the barns. Cathy had a crazed grin on her face and was carrying two bloody knives.

The knives put paid to Sylvia's plans to confront the girl. She ducked back into the doorway and waited until Cathy vanished around the side of the farmhouse before stepping out again.

This time her flight was delayed for a different reason. The DJ, Amy Fox, had just burst out of the border of the sunflower field and was running for her life, with two of the monsters in hot pursuit. Amy's silver-blonde hair was streaming in the wind. She had a good head start but the black creatures were gaining on her. Their red eyes glowed like vehicle brake lights. They had a strange way of running, as if they were swimming through the air. Sometimes their feet seemed not to touch the ground. The monsters didn't appear to move fast, but this was deceptive. They'd already halved the distance between themselves and Amy Fox.

Pursued and pursuer ran past the barns and vanished into the night-draped forest.

Sylvia turned her mind back to her own plight.

I'd better get a move on before they find me too.

"Hi, cousin!"

Sylvia's heart seemed to leap into her mouth. She spun around. Cathy was slashing at her with a knife. The teenager must have run around the house. She was approaching Sylvia from the very direction in which she intended to flee.

"Die!" Cathy said gleefully. "Die!" Now her white mask had splashes of blood on it.

Sylvia ducked in the nick of time. The red blade missed her neck.

But now Sylvia panicked. She forgot her resolve to save her friends. All that filled her thoughts now was survival. How to save herself. She evaded two more swipes of Cathy's knives, then ran out into the night. She ran towards the barns, in the same direction that the DJ and her hellish pursuers had vanished.

Maybe, just maybe, there was safety that way.

While fleeing, she looked back to see if Cathy was coming after her. Cathy was laughing at her, waving her bloody knives in the night. But no, she wasn't following.

Relieved, Sylvia turned back to her flight. But then she caught a sudden glimpse of something large lying in her path, missed her footing, and fell over it.

She hit the ground hard, but was unhurt. She was about leaping to her feet again—she'd already made it up to her hands and knees—when she got a good glimpse of what she'd fallen over.

It was her boyfriend's corpse. Barry lay there, his eyes open, a horrible bloody gash in his neck.

The sight transfixed Sylvia as if she'd been nailed to the ground. Then nausea overcame her and she began puking.

She was still throwing up when the smell of burning surrounded her. The smell of burning air. The smell of burning sunflowers. The smell of burning people.

Sylvia realized that the creatures had caught her. And behind them she heard Cathy's laughter.

Still she tried to escape. She leapt to her feet but was restrained by a flaming hand gripping her right wrist. She screamed, vomit flying unheeded from her mouth. They grabbed her left wrist too and her pain doubled. She swooned, but was unable to completely lose consciousness. The pain kept her awake.

A stupefied thought ran through Sylvia's mind: *Aw, man, this has gotta be the worst birthday anyone's ever had.*

Next, she was lifted off her feet by red-hot hands and carried off somewhere. Her haze of pain was surrounded by the stench of melting fabric and burning flesh. Through her agony she realized that the roasting she smelt was the smell of her own burning body.

CHAPTER 15

Ben

Snort and Liza weren't yet back with the shovels.

Ben didn't know what to make of it. He estimated they'd been gone for half an hour now. Though Ben wasn't in any hurry to be buried alive, he found the delay disturbing. Being bound and gagged and abandoned in a deep hole out in a dark forest was unnerving enough, even without the planned homicide. A freak flash flood filling his hole with water would be sufficient to kill him.

Escape from his hole was still totally of the question. It was taking all of his willpower just to keep standing. And now bugs had begun investigating his naked body. Some of them were even biting him. Their bites felt like pins being stuck into him.

Whatever the hell did they shoot me up with? Horse tranks?

The more tired he felt, the harder it was to think.

Still he tried: *Something's keeping them from coming back. Maybe Snort switched Liza's suggestion around and they're peddling drugs over at that party before coming to kill me.*

But that was the other odd thing: the distant party seemed to have died. And very abruptly too. Since the music had stopped just after Snort and Liza left him to go fetch the shovels, it hadn't started up again.

I thought I heard screaming, but then it died out too and . . .

At that moment Ben heard approaching noises. His heart instantly lurched with fear.

They're back. I'm dead! I'm a goner. I'm . . .

But something didn't sound right. For one thing, Snort and Liza weren't talking. And also, there was this odd smell of burning. Like charred meat. Meat so burnt it was indistinguishable from coal, but letting off reminiscent vapors of its past life.

Ben forced himself up on tiptoe and peeked out of the hole.

There were two humanoid creatures approaching. Though it was almost pitch-black beneath the trees, the creatures were easy to make out because they both glowed with a reddish-orange light that spilled from cracks up and down their bodies.

Both creatures also had glowing red eyes.

Like walking lanterns, Ben thought.

The closer they got to Ben's pit, the easier they were to see. He could also feel the heat they gave off. It felt as if they were burning. Except for their glowing eyes and the light spilling from within them, their bodies seemed blacker than the night itself.

They moved forward with focus, not looking Ben's way at all. They were clearly headed somewhere beyond the woods, somewhere on the farm.

Then Ben realized that each creature was dragging something behind it.

Very carefully (because now he smelt blood in the air too, which alerted him that these things were dangerous), he tried to make out what the two black creatures were pulling after them.

Bodies. Two dead human bodies.

Ben identified the corpses from their clothes, because both of their heads were missing: Snort's and Liza's decapitated bodies.

Feeling a massive surge of mingled relief and terror, Ben let himself down from his tiptoed position. He stood on his feet for a moment longer, then let himself down to the bottom of the pit.

He sat there trembling, uncertain if his problems were over or if they'd just increased in magnitude.

CHAPTER 16

Sharon & Vanni @
No. 146 Corey Street, West Roxbury, Boston

That same night, at 10:00 p.m., in the living room of the Donnelly residence, Michael Donnelly kissed his wife Sharon, then waved to their next door neighbor Vanni Warren.

He grinned. "Alright, girls, I'll be back in a half-hour or so. Be good now."

Then, carrying he and Sharon's sleeping 5-year-old son Davey, he headed for the door.

"Hey, honey, tell Ann I'll call her from the farm tomorrow," Sharon called after him.

He nodded back. "Will do."

Ann was Michael's sister. She lived up in Boston's North End district. Michael was off to drop Davey with her for the weekend.

He should have done it earlier in the day, but both he and Sharon had been busy all afternoon. The other option was to drop the child off on their drive out to the party, but as its name implied, North End was up north and they were headed west. This wouldn't have made much difference, but Vanni's husband Darrin was in the office working late and there was no point keeping Ann awake till they were ready to leave, when her nephew was already sound asleep.

Michael exited. Sharon and Vanni waited until they heard the sound of his car departing, then grinned at one another across the living room. "You think we've got enough time before they both get back?" Vanni asked.

"Definitely," Sharon replied her. "My biological clock assures me that we do."

The wives got up, locked the front door, and hand-in-hand, proceeded into Sharon's bedroom.

A few seconds later, both were naked and Vanni was pushing Sharon backwards onto the bed.

***

As always when they did this, Sharon felt a brief twinge of conscience: *Oh, we're both cheating on our husbands. We really shouldn't!*

But then Vanni's soft lips were pressing hard on hers and she surrendered to the fire burning in her groin. (Vanni was usually the dominant partner when they made love.) It helped that Vanni was so expert at exciting her, knowing exactly how and where to tease her to elicit the most devastating sexual responses.

Once sexual biology took over, the mind stood little chance of resistance.

Now, Vanni licked her down, her wet tongue making a snail-trail from the hollow of Sharon's neck, to her left nipple, sucking hard on it, then across to her right nipple, more hard sucking, then down, down, down to her crotch. She worked her tongue so slowly that Sharon felt as if time had stopped. Eternity was herself poised on the verge of orgasm. She was a bomb with a paused clitoral timer.

When Vanni's lips fastened on her clitoris, she rose to an instant climax. Conscious that their men could return unannounced, Sharon chewed on her thumb to keep from shrieking out her pleasure.

Vanni sank fingers into Sharon's sex and licked her to two more orgasms. Then she sat up. "Do me too," she gasped, then lay on her back.

Sharon's body was still trembling from her last climax. She lay on Vanni and worked her sex with her left hand, dipping fingers into the dripping vagina, stroking the erect clitoris. Vanni gasped. Sharon kissed her; her cheeks, her eyes; finally her lips. She sucked her tongue like she wanted to dry it out. She moved her mouth lower and nibbled on Vanni's stiff nipples.

Vanni began trembling, began coming too.

***

"I feel guiltier each time," Sharon said afterward. "But it's sweeter each time too."

"I know what you mean, darling," Vanni said, kissing her on the nose. "Personally, the more of you I get, the more of you I want."

"Are we in love?"

"Maybe, but I don't think so. I love your body, and I seriously love having sex with you, but . . ."

"Yeah, I know. I'm in love with Michael, and yet . . ."

Finding it difficult to express their forbidden feelings, the lustful pair kissed and cuddled some more.

CHAPTER 17

Family Ties

The Warrens lived right next door to the Donnellys, at No. 144 Corey Street. All four of them, husbands and wives, were the best of friends with each other.

The two families did most things together.

Though both wives were beautiful women, they were physical opposites.

Sharon Donnelly was petite, with long black hair and blue eyes. She had naturally large breasts, which childbirth had doubled in size.

On the other hand, Vanessa 'Vanni' Warren was tall and slim and blonde, with hot lips and gorgeous gray eyes.

In contrast to this, their husbands looked like brothers—both men were of average height and weight, had chestnut-brown hair and eyes and were passably good-looking, with Darrin Warren the taller by two inches.

Career-wise, Michael Donnelly was a successful realtor.

Sharon had started off her professional life as Michael's secretary, then gotten pregnant with Davey and successfully changed her career arc to housewifery. She was currently working on having a second baby.

Darrin was a senior systems analyst with Ellis Drake Incorporated.

For the most part, Vanni Warren was a bored trophy wife. She'd initially worked in a library, but had grown tired of being surrounded by books. At the moment, inspired by Sharon, she too was trying to get pregnant, while doing some eBay trading on the side. The eBay thing was mostly a distraction though. They didn't need the extra money. Darrin earned enough to pay her two salaries if she insisted on it.

All four of them were in their late twenties.

They all knew Sylvia Stewart, whose birthday party they were off to attend.

Sylvia had started off as Sharon's high school friend, then had met Darrin at work; then Sharon and Darrin had each independently introduced her to their respective spouses.

After which, the house next door to the Donelly's had come up for sale. Joanna Wilson, the woman who'd lived there, had died after her daughter cut both of her feet off.

So, on Michael's recommendation, the Warrens had moved house from the nearby town of Quincy to the Boston suburb of West Roxbury.

Where, a lot later, both couples had discovered over cocktails that they both knew Sylvia Stewart and that they'd both been invited to her 30th birthday celebration.

Everyone loved Sylvia and wanted to attend. And what was more natural than best friends (and best family friends, for that matter) attending together?

And tonight was the big night.

CHAPTER 18

Sharon & Michael & Vanni & Darrin

"Any luck getting Sylvia on the phone?" Vanni asked Sharon as they both repaired their makeup.

Before replying, Sharon checked that the bed was properly made. Michael wasn't likely to come in for anything on his return, but if he did there mustn't be any telltale signs.

"None," she said after deciding the bed looked okay. "It's still like Michael said earlier, like there's an AT&T blackout over there—just this crazy buzz like the phone's about to blow up in my ear." She shrugged. "It's a good thing her uncle's farm is easy to find."

She shifted her attention to her clothes, checking them for telltale creases. Her denim pants were fine, but her green top had some red lipstick on it. She ditched the blouse in the laundry basket and got out a pink top as replacement.

Vanni smirked. "Ha ha. At least *she says* it's easy to find. I'd hate for us to be driving around at midnight trying one deserted access road after the other, and waking up a succession of increasingly irate farmers with shotguns. No telling when one of them'll be mad enough to take a shot at us."

Unlike Sharon, Vanni felt no unease concerning her appearance. Her own clothes hadn't creased up: she was wearing blue stretch pants, and a red leather jacket over a pink/gray Ambient Godfathers tee shirt. Like Sharon though, she too was wearing high heels. Hopefully, they wouldn't be dancing in the mud.

Two suitcases of spare clothes for both couples were already packed in the trunk of the Donnelly's SUV.

They shared a last romantic hug, not kissing now so as not to smear their lipstick, then returned to the living room. Sharon unlocked the front door. They sat on different chairs and smiled cool, sated smiles at each other.

"Michael should be getting back any moment soon," Sharon mused. She got up and pirouetted. "How do I look?"

"Delicious enough to eat again. But we've no time. The boys *are* back."

Sharon too heard the sound of the car pulling up the drive. She walked to the front windows and parted the drapes.

"It's Michael," she called back to Vanni, ". . . and Darrin's just pulling into your driveway too. They must've met up somewhere."

Michael pushed open the front door and grinned at them. "Alright, my male offspring is now safely deposited with my female sibling. So, are you two beauties ready to party?"

"We sure are, man."

Then he dashed past them. "I gotta pee. See you outside in the ride."

"That's men for you," Sharon whispered to Vanni as they exited the door, "he didn't even notice that I changed my top."

In response, Vanni smacked her bottom hard. Then she walked over to kiss her own husband welcome. Darrin Warren was walking over from their front porch.

"Hi, honey, how was work today?"

Darrin felt her ass and mock-groaned. "Oh, so, so. Thank God I can finally start the weekend. I've forewarned that butt-kisser Mason that I'm not working any more Saturdays for at least another month. He can have Harriman do it." In the short interval since arriving home, Darrin had switched clothes, discarding his work suit for tee shirt, jeans and hush puppies.

Vanni snuggled up against him. "Oh, forget work, honey. It's time to party, ain't it?"

"Oh, yeah, it sure is." Darrin grinned, then squinted at Sharon. "Where's Michael got to?"

She shrugged and grinned back. "Man business."

Michael stepped out of the house then. "Alright, folks," he growled, punching the air, "now let's get this damn show on the damn road!"

They piled into the Donnelly's black Audi Q5 SUV and headed out of town, with Darrin at the wheel.

"Did either of you guys have any luck getting Sylvia on the phone?" Sharon asked after a while.

"Yeah," Vanni seconded. "Or anyone else over there?"

"Not a ghost," Darrin replied, turning off Worcester Road and looping into the cloverleaf interchange onto the I-90 Interstate. "Just that crazy hum like your ears are melting. But then, Sylvia already told us all that the phone reception over there is messed up anyway."

"We'll get us there, girls," Michael said. "Don't panic, the Massachusetts road network has never before defeated a husband on a mission to get recreationally wasted. Now, how 'bout sharing out some of those beers?"

"Yeah, let's have some beers," Darrin agreed.

Vanni got cold beers out of the icebox on the backseat and passed them around.

"None for you, darling," she told her husband, handing him a Monster Energy drink instead. "I'll never forgive you if you crash this ride and kill me before you've gotten me pregnant."

CHAPTER 19

Ronan

Ronan Higgins had never imagined people had so much blood in them.

Or that it was so much work cutting them up.

He straightened up now and considered the naked corpse on the workbench. One of Sylvia's male friends. He almost remembered this one's name. Was it Larry or Barry or Harry or Gary? It was hard to tell when the top of the guy's head was missing and his brains had dripped forward over his face. And that wasn't Ronan's doing; it was how the 'red-eyes' had delivered the corpse to him.

He tried matching the man's clothes to one of the cars. White Toyota SUV or black Ford sedan or that BMW convertible? No luck there either. The dead man remained anonymous.

Ronan leaned on his axe and wiped sweat from his brow. It didn't matter who the man was. Ronan was halfway done with chopping him up. Both of the man's legs were already in red pieces in a large metal tub, along with his arms and all of his innards.

That was another thing. Ronan was also surprised by how much guts people had in them. Seemingly miles of guts. Wet and slimy and glistening. He surveyed the other tubs he'd already filled with chunks of dead people—four in all. The viscera in those glistened redly too. Most of the blood from the bodies was on the floor, drained away along whichever cracks in the concrete it had found accessible.

The axe was stained red now. Ronan was satisfied. There was almost enough meat to start the planting.

He was tired from all the hacking, but not much so. The Bargainer had promised him strength to carry out his task, and he'd kept his promise. He'd given Ronan something to drink that had filled him with a horrible, devilish energy, so that now it was harder for him to rest than to butcher the bodies.

Okay, he decided, *time to finish this one.*

He resumed work. Before chopping the man's torso into bits, he first expertly split the remnants of his head. At first cutting up heads had proved tricky—the novice Ronan had left them till last, and then they'd tended to roll off the workbench if not hit dead-center—but he'd now gotten the hang of it. The trick was to chop them up while they were still attached to the body, that way the head was anchored in place no matter how sideways you hit it.

Once the man was completely dismantled, Ronan scooped his remains into the metal tub and walked over to the corpse pile to fetch another one.

Cathy was busy undressing the corpses. She was sitting on a wood stump and snipping their clothes off with scissors. Once they were naked, she would then roll them over towards her father.

To one side of the corpse pile was a smaller, rising heap of wallets and purses. Cathy, always an enterprising young woman, had hit on the idea of looting the corpses' money. "They don't need it where they've gone," she'd said.

Ronan agreed with her. You couldn't take it with you. Might as well spend it on their dead behalves.

"How you makin' out so far?" he asked her. He found her black-on-whiteface murder-clown makeup very appropriate for tonight.

She nodded back, all splattered with blood, hair inclusive. "Two thousand dollars. Enough to buy me a new wardrobe."

He smiled. "That's my girl."

Ronan felt pleased, at peace with himself. Most of this good feeling came from just seeing Cathy alive again. Watching her cut the clothes off the corpses with her scissors, all seemed well with his world.

The barn was filled with the reek of rare-cooked human steak.

He looked over at the pile of dead people. There were about fifteen of them stacked here, and the red-eyes were still bringing more in, each additional dumping announced by the fire-demons' brimstone stink. About half of the dead had no eyes. Ten or so had their faces completely burned away, melted and scarred to erasure by the red-eyes' flaming fingers. Their clothes too were singed in patches from the red-eyes' heat.

Ronan anticipated at least ten more corpses shortly arriving. Meaning he had at least twenty-five stiffs to get through. To cut through. They all had to be chopped up and set in tubs for the Bargainer's seeds. It would be a hard night's work, but strong as he felt after drinking that devil's elixir the Bargainer had given him, Ronan felt he could take on the world.

His fevered fanatical gaze moved from the corpses to his nubile daughter. Feeling the start of an erection, he squeezed his crotch.

Too bad that Cathy was his daughter. For some reason, hacking up all these bodies was making him horny. At the moment he'd give anything for a woman to sleep with.

Doin' the Devil's work makes one think the Devil's thoughts, it seems.

He spat at the pleasant thought, then bent and gripped one of the female corpses by her ankle.

Should I fuck her? The thought flickered through Ronan's mind, its initial weak spark quickly growing in tempting intensity. Ronan quashed the urge before it became a blaze. No, he wasn't about having sex with any corpses. Cathy wouldn't stand for it, for one thing. For another, most of these dead women looked like shit now, whatever prettiness they'd had whilst alive seemingly leeched from their corpses by the very terror of their dying; and whatever comeliness fear hadn't stolen, the red-eyes' flaming fingers had.

An acrid stink of burning air announced a red-eye's arrival. Ronan watched the black creature fling another corpse up onto the morbid pile, then turn and stalk off, its eyes glowing saucers, its gait evil and forbidding because, though not cloven-hoofed, its feet nonetheless only had two fat toes.

The rest of the red-eyes were either scavenging for the rest of the dead or were busy hiding the dead folks' vehicles and belongings. The creatures were also covering the blood they'd spilled with sand. When the police turned up, as they were certain to do, there must be no signs of foul play anywhere.

The red-eye stalked out the barn door. Ronan peered beyond the walking ebon nightmare, out into the dusky night. Lots of stars.

He looked inside again, at the piled corpses, wondering where in their midst his niece Sylvia was. He thought he'd seen the red-eyes bring her in with the rest, but wasn't sure.

"Hey, Cathy," he asked, "have you seen your cousin anywhere?"

"Sylvia?" She pointed at the stacked bodies. "She's part of the pile somewhere. It's hard to tell who's who with all those burn marks on them."

Ronan looked worried for a minute. "Girl, are you sure she's in there? You're certain she didn't get away? It'll be a huge mess for us if she's escaped. The Bargainer won't like it one bit."

"Aw, stop worrying, dad. The red-eyes got her. I was there. I saw them kill her."

Ronan nodded. "Okay, then. Just remember the Bargainer warned us to be careful. He can fix some things for us, but we gotta be alert on our own too. He can't be everywhere at once."

"Uncle Bargainer sure is strange, dad."

"Yes, he really is."

Cathy waved a handful of hundreds at Ronan.

"Five hundred bucks more. Everyone here is just loaded!" She flung the raided wallet on top of the others and began snipping off the man's pants.

Ronan, about to chop off his new corpse's legs, was surprised when Cathy suddenly burst into tears.

"What's wrong with you, girl?"

She continued crying, the black circles around her eyes dripping down her whitened face like wet mascara.

"I just feel so weird, daddy," she wept. "I dislike how I'm enjoying all this killing so much. I know it's necessary and it's actually great fun. But . . . but . . . every so often I just feel so sad for them—all these dead people. But I'm really happy and glad at the same time."

Ronan couldn't bear to see her sad. Oh, he loved his little girl so much.

He set down the axe and went and cuddled her.

"Now now, darling. You just remember what we're doing this for. It's an exchange. Something for something."

While speaking, he hugged her close and stroked her bloody hair. At first she resisted him, her body hard and trembling against his, but slowly she relaxed against him and began giggling. She wiped her eyes dry.

Ronan let go of her when he felt his penis growing hard again.

Dammit! What's the matter with my dick?

He returned quickly to his workbench, retrieved the axe from the floor, and lopped off both of the dead woman's feet with loud, resounding clunks. Working didn't deaden his arousal, but it took his mind off it. He systematically shattered the corpse's leg bones with a sledgehammer, split them into red chunks of meat and gristle and bone with the axe, and scooped them into a fresh tub. He dropped the axe and picked up a long knife. With this he slit the woman open from chest to navel and began hauling out her guts.

He found it weird how even a woman this small was full of guts. She was big-bellied and packed with intestines. And her intestines seemed packed full of poop. Fertilizer for demon seeds.

Cathy meanwhile, resumed stripping and looting the corpses. Her father couldn't see it, but under her garish makeup her face was flushed with sexual desire. She felt aroused enough to melt from the craving. Since her resurrection Cathy Higgins had been feeling almost perpetually aroused. She'd been masturbating a lot, wishing she had a boy around to seduce. She'd even fantasized about doing it with her father. But of course she wouldn't—that would be gross.

Outwardly she maintained a calm front. But she needed a guy to bed and soon. Or else, only Heaven . . . no . . . only Hell knew what she'd resort to doing.

Father and daughter worked on. Except for the regular sounds of gruesome butchery, they worked in silence, happy to be near one another.

Every once in a while, one of the red-eyes would arrive with either a fresh corpse or parts of one.

After a while, Ronan decided to take a breather. He stopped chopping the bodies and began planting the seeds instead.

This was simple enough to do: he just pulled each filled tub to a prearranged spot in the barn and dropped a seed in its middle. Then he pushed the seed inward, down to about the center of the butchered meat and left it in there.

The Bargainer had told Ronan these seeds would grow really fast. Ronan was eager to see what their plants would look like.

His anticipation was natural. He was, after all, a farmer. A farmer right to his now completely corrupted core.

CHAPTER 20

Ben

Ben dreamt.

Whether influenced by the cocktail of drugs in his system, or whether by the evil that had now taken root in the earth of the Higgins Farm and was seeping into him unawares, his dreaming had a surreal quality to it that would have made Max Ernst proud.

Ben saw a tall, tall, TALL man in black cowboy clothes with a face like Johnny Cash if Cash had had some Mexican blood in him, but a face as old as time and more lined than the US roadmap, walking through an Earth that had stopped spinning. An Earth with a permanent dayside and nightside. Forces of immense darkness were responsible for the world's static state, wizardry so vile that even dreaming about it broke Ben out in a cold sweat. And here on this Static Earth, monsters that men had consigned to the realm of myth and legend lived and breathed with as much birthright as humankind.

The immensely tall man with the wizened face was a negotiator of some kind—his job was making bargains. And this time, he'd made a deal with a creature named Underboss, a nightside being so immensely evil that even its peers shunned it. Underboss looked like a cross between a snail and a crocodile. It was a walking mass of pestilence, with creating chaos as its purpose. It existed solely to generate confusion and misery for mankind. Underboss claimed it had escaped from Hell, but some Static Earth wizards and witches claimed it was still on Satan's payroll.

Ben didn't hear much of what the pair discussed, just scraps of talk that made no sense to him.

At a point Underboss said, "I already asked your younger brother, but he declined."

"Oh, the Fixer's a goody two-shoes," the TALL man drolly replied. "In keeping with his name he prefers repair jobs, whilst I . . ."

Finally, however, the nauseating creature handed the tall, TALL man a pouch of seeds.

"Plant these," the horrible thing said in its gurgling voice. "Harvest them successfully and Masochist State can have its peace."

The TALL man studied the pouch for a long moment. Then he replied Underboss in some amusement: "Did I hear you say 'Plant?'"

"Yes, *plant*. The problem?"

"I make deals. I'm no farmer."

"Then *find* a farmer. An expert and reliable one. No germination means no next generations for your clients. One touch of a button and . . ."

"Where the hell am I supposed . . . ?"

Underboss laughed nastily. Before speaking again it rolled around a little, up and down the walls of its disgusting cavern and back and forth across the space's ceiling.

Then it returned to the ground and after more foul laugher, said, "The solution is simple: go to the Spinning Earth. There are plenty of farmers there." Yet more laughter followed. "In fact, I suggest you go to the same place as you would here to find a farmer. Right back where you started this quest—your clients. I believe that on our duplicate planet, Masochist State is called Massachusetts."

Ben's dream ended with the impossibly TALL man who looked a wizened Mexican version of Johnny Cash (if Johnny Cash had been ten feet tall) musing on that solution.

CHAPTER 21

Sharon & Michael & Vanni & Darrin

"The Massachusetts countryside sucks penis at night," Vanni said with a pout. "One of you husbands tell us a story to pass the time."

"Yeah," Sharon agreed after a sip of beer. "Something interesting. I don't wanna hear any gossip from your offices about who's now left his wife for his secretary."

"I can't think of anything," Darrin said from behind the SUV's wheel. "I live a placid easy life which Vanni does her best to disrupt."

"Stop pretending you dislike the disruptions," Vanni giggled back. "Most times people can hear you gasping and begging me for more disruption all the way down the street."

Darrin swerved the heavy Audi SUV left, then laughed. "Sometimes I wonder what the hell I was looking for in the library the day I met you."

"Sex?" Sharon teased. "Librarians reputedly have intelligent pussies."

"Yeah," Vanni quickly agreed. "It's how we trap bookworms."

Michael laughed. He leaned over between the front seats so he could see the women in the back. "Alright, enough, fellow travelers. Let me entertain you. Permit me to tell you the tale of House No. 666."

Vanni made a face. "House No. 666? I ain't sure I wanna hear about this."

"Too late," Michael said. "You girls requested a story and you're gonna get it."

"This is like made-up, right . . . right, baby?" Sharon asked.

Her husband shook his head. "No, no . . . no. No. 666 Converse Street is an actual house in Springfield that the owners want to sell, but which no one wants to buy."

"I'd buy it," Darrin said. "I ain't into that superstitious BS."

"I assure you, dear best friend, that you don't want this house."

Darrin sniggered. "Oh yeah? What's the gimmick here? It's a gateway to Hell or where the Antichrist is supposed to be born?"

The SUV sped on along I-90. The night was warm, welcoming even. None of the four travelers had the slightest inkling that they were speeding towards tragedy.

"So," Sharon prompted, "out with the tale, man. What's so special about this house then?"

Michael shook his head again. "Nothing *that* spectacular. Just that everyone who's ever lived there—every single tenant—has died an inexplicable death. And usually within a year of their moving into the place.

Vanni yawned. "Oh, how boring. Examples?"

Michael's face now took on a disquieted expression. "Guys, this isn't any kind of a joking matter. There's city records of the people dying in there."

"For real, baby?" his wife asked.

"Yeah. When I visited the premises, I felt so spooked that I was gonna turn down the owners' request to sell it for them. But . . . it's a huge commission."

"I'll buy it," Darrin said. "That way you'll get the huge commission."

Michael shook his head emphatically. "Man, I already told you—you don't want this house."

"But I do. I really do. Just imagine holding Vanni's next birthday party there. We'll rename it 'Vanessa Warren's Spooky Mansion.' "

"Don't you dare," Vanni growled. She got out fresh beers and handed them around. Darrin glanced back pleading at her. She ignored his pleading, handed him a Red Bull instead. "Now you've gotten me interested," she told Michael. "Tell us some of the stories. How exactly did the tenants die?"

"On the surface, it's all accidents." He shot a brief glance over the top of the seat at his wife. "Babe, you following this?"

"Yes, yes, I am," she replied, an immersed look on her face.

"Okay, then. See, the last guy shot himself in the head—by accident . . ."

***

Sharon actually wasn't paying any attention to Michael's story. She was doing her utmost to have a quiet orgasm.

Unseen and unsuspected by either husband, Vanni had her fingers down inside Sharon's pants and was masturbating her. This was possible because the icebox on the backseat that contained the drinks had been placed behind the driver's seat. Vanni was sitting in the middle so she could see out of the windshield. Sharon was seated behind Michael.

Darrin couldn't see what the women were doing because he was watching the road. Michael couldn't see them because he was concentrating on his story and because Vanni was in the way.

It was up to Sharon to relax and come in the dark vehicle interior without giving the game away.

"And," Michael went on, "the previous tenant—a schoolteacher—drowned in the bathtub."

Sharon relaxed as Vanni's fingers slid deeper down, into her sex. Wow! This was triply thrilling: firstly, there was the barebones sexual sensation; then there was the throbbing of the luxury car they were riding in—doing it in the moving SUV felt like being inside of a massive vibrator; then there was the additional thrill of danger, the knowledge that if she gasped or moaned they'd be caught.

"Seriously?" Darrin laughed. "You hearing this, honey?"

Vanni nodded. "Yeah, that makes two. But that ain't too bad, is it? It could still be coincidence." She dug her fingers deeper into Sharon's vagina and twisted them. She felt her lady lover's body tense from the pleasure she couldn't express. She giggled. Her only worry was that the smell of sex might alert the guys to what was happening. She sipped her beer coolly, blithely assuming the alcoholic odor would smother the erotic one.

"Oh, there's more," Michael went on.

Darrin smirked and tapped the steering wheel. "We're listening, dude."

"Keep listening." He frowned. "The couple who lived there before that—husband and wife in their sixties—both fell down the stairs and broke their necks a week apart from each other."

"Alright, now *that's* creepy," Vanni agreed while jerking her fingers in and out of Sharon's vagina. Then, thinking about what she'd just heard, she stopped rubbing Sharon's clitoris for a moment. Sharon instantly forced her fingers back into motion.

"Wow—that's much too coincidental to be a coincidence!" Sharon gasped, relieved to be able to release some of the pleasure pressure.

"Man, I'm beginning to think you should stop telling this tale," Vanni said.

"Hell no, honey," her husband countered, "I wanna hear the rest of it. I'm still not convinced the house is jinxed."

Vanni shut up and continued masturbating Sharon. Darrin concentrated on the road. Sharon concentrated on coming quietly.

"Alright," Michael said. "Five years before that, there was the case of the guy who hung himself while sleepwalking."

"Hey!" Darrin said. "Dude, get your facts straight: Okay, so the guy committed suicide. But how could they know he'd done it while sleepwalking?"

"The neighbor lady saw him from her window. The old girl woke up for a glass of water at 2 a.m., saw the guy with a blank look on his face and assumed nothing was wrong. It wasn't the first time—she was used to him pacing in the night. It was only in the morning that they discovered his corpse."

"That's just creepy," Vanni agreed, pleasuring Sharon now completely forgotten. "Just imagine that guy walking downstairs and slipping a noose around his own neck without even realizing he was doing so, and then—"

"Shit!" Sharon gasped, her orgasm hitting her at that exact instant. She'd taken over where Vanni left off and stroked herself over the edge. She fought to tame her sexualized voice: "Alright . . . I'm . . . I'm . . . utterly satisfied now . . . that that house is weird."

"Me too," Vanni said gently. She withdrew her hand from Sharon's pants. A moment later, she felt Sharon wiping her fingers dry with a tissue.

"So," Michael asked Darrin, "how 'bout it, buddy? You still in the market for House No. 666? I'll make you a good price."

"I don't know," Darrin said. They'd arrived at the outskirts of the town of Chester, close to the Higgins Farm. According to the GPS, they were about reaching their destination. Darrin had slowed down so he didn't mistake one dark turnoff road for another. "Sure it's a scary tale. But, come on, man, coincidences do happen."

"Ah, the skeptic," Michael groaned with a shrug. "Alright, if you need more convincing, let me tell you the story of another set of residents. This happened fifteen years back. Okay, so . . ."

"We don't wanna hear it!" Vanni and Sharon both shrieked. "And, darling," Vanni added, "please discard any suicidal notions you've got about buying the damn place."

"Aw, c'mon, honey. It'll be good for us. Just imagine Halloween in such a house."

"Forget it, baby. No spooky house for us."

Michael grinned at Darrin. "Sometimes, it pays to have a superstitious wife. Trust me, she's just saved both your lives."

He accepted a beer from Vanni, then leaned back into his seat, asking Darrin: "We there yet, dude?"

"In five minutes or so. Some of these damn back roads don't have signs on 'em."

Behind them, Vanni leaned over on Sharon, whose breathing had now returned to normal. She rested her head on the smaller woman's larger breasts.

"That was incredible," Sharon whispered to Vanni. "Just incredible."

"I know," Vanni whispered back. "Someone did it to me once. I was fourteen and my parents were driving me and a girlfriend to summer camp in Connecticut. They were listening to the radio and she began playing with me behind their backs. It was intense. Bottled up and couldn't let out a peep, or else . . . It was . . . put it like this—I screamed when I came."

"You did?"

"Uh huh. My dad drove off the road in shock. He and my mom were scared shitless. I lied to them that I'd felt a sudden sharp pain in my belly. The fact that I had tears streaming down my cheeks from the pleasure convinced them I was really hurting."

"Hey, what are you girls whispering about back there?" Michael asked. "C'mon, let's smell your dirty female laundry too."

Sharon laughed. "Oh, it's actually nothing, darling. Just girl stuff. Vanni's reminiscing on a ride she once took that was similar to this one."

CHAPTER 22

Next Door Sex Detour

The affair between Sharon Donnelly and Vanni Warren began one bright April morning. That spring morning, Vanni had suddenly realized she hadn't enough sugar at home to bake her intended cherry cake and had phoned Sharon, asking if she could borrow some.

"Sure," Sharon had replied. She'd added that she was just about having a shower, but that she'd leave the kitchen door open. Vanni could just walk in.

Vanni walked in. She sat in the living room and waited awhile. When Sharon hadn't appeared after ten minutes, a slightly worried Vanni walked into the bathroom looking for her.

She'd found Sharon masturbating in the shower, eyes closed, hand between her legs, gently moaning while the hot water rained on her.

Vanni loved her husband. She'd never once cheated on Darrin. Neither did she plan on doing so. But seeing Sharon there that morning, her little body and large motherly breasts dripping with lust and water, something kindled inside her.

Not bothering to undress first, she'd slipped into the shower and begun sucking on Sharon's nipples.

Sharon had jerked alert with fright.

"Relax, it's only me," Vanni had soothed. "Darling, I believe from now on we're gonna be breast friends."

Sharon had stood there, uncertain of what she should be doing. Should she run or should she stay and play along? All of a sudden she really wanted to play.

Aware of her confusion, Vanni had winked. "Go back to doing what I interrupted. I mean, playing with yourself. I'm just gonna help you along." Then she'd dropped her lips back to sucking on Sharon's breasts. A few seconds later, Sharon had resumed masturbating. This time she gripped Vanni's head with her free hand and pressed it firmly against her chest.

After Sharon's orgasm, they'd both dried off, and then Vanni had taken Sharon into the bedroom and taught her the intricacies of satisfying another woman in bed.

***

Things had developed since then. They made love most mornings when Sharon's son was in kindergarten.

Vanni had discovered that Sharon was very kinky. She liked playing dress up. She also liked trying out different kinds of sexual positions. Strap-ons, dildos, everything. Vanni often wondered how Michael coped with her ceaseless demands for sexual experimentation.

Sharon also seemed more emotionally involved in their relationship. To Vanni, their affair was just fun, something other than shopping to spice up the otherwise boring day of a wealthy suburban housewife. But Sharon was continually professing her love for Vanni, and hinting that if she and Michael didn't have their son Davey, she'd gladly ditch her marriage so she and Vanni could be together for real.

Vanni didn't see it that way. She was happy in her own marriage; she was smart enough to realize there wasn't anything she wasn't getting with Darrin that she'd find outside.

Besides, she didn't want a fulltime lesbian partner. And it wasn't just considerations of social ostracization and needing to slot into a minority subculture that she was wary of.

In Vanni's experience, dating other women was just too much hard work. Two females emoting at each other all the time. Vanni felt the reason why women fit so well together with men was because men were emotional sponges: they sucked up what you threw at them and, like black holes, threw very little back. Women complained about that, but that very difference was the glue that held the sexes together. With two women, both were 'throwing' all the time and neither was absorbing anything; and so, except for their issues with men that prevented their seeking satisfaction in that direction, there was really nothing keeping them together.

You had to actually 'feel' lesbian to do lesbian right; or else you felt really *wrong*; and Vanni didn't 'feel' lesbian. She didn't dislike men enough to want to permanently be with a woman. She didn't dislike men at all.

Nor, she suspected, did Sharon. As far as she could see, Sharon was happily married too. She was just bored, and fantasized that the thrill of their sexual games could actually translate into greener pastures.

Vanni knew it wouldn't. They both had it too good to throw away over some idle sapphic fancy. Vanni had no intention of going back to work in a library and slaving away to pay the bills for Sharon and her son.

She intended to drum that reality into Sharon's beautiful head.

CHAPTER 23

Ronan & Cathy

"Hey, dad," Cathy called out suddenly, "Sylvia's still alive."

Ronan stopped hacking away at a fat man's body. "What? She is?"

"See for yourself."

He looked. Sure enough, there was his niece Sylvia Stewart on the floor, lying on her back with her chest rising and falling gently. She was out cold. She had lots of burn marks on her arms and legs, particularly on her wrists. Her clothes were charred in places, as if they had caught fire while the red-eyes were bringing her in.

Sylvia seemed to be the last of the partygoers being readied for the chopping block. Cathy had stripped all the rest—about eight or ten corpses.

"She wasn't the first they brought in, so how . . . ?" Ronan asked.

"I think she rolled down when I pulled some others out," Cathy explained. Then her brow creased up. "Hey, dad, are you gonna chop her up like the rest?"

He shook his head. "I can't. She's family."

Cathy looked unconvinced. "She'll tell on us if she gets away."

Shit, Ronan thought, staring at the unconscious young woman. *What am I gonna do with her? I don't wanna kill the girl.*

He watched Sylvia's chest lift and drop and felt his penis twitch with excitement. She had great breasts. He began getting an erection.

He shook his head and turned away from the sight.

Oh no, I ain't doing that!

But then the Devil entered into Ronan Higgins and all consideration of good, pity and mercy left him. He nodded to his daughter. "You're right, honey. She'll run straight to the cops if we let her go. So we need to see to it that she doesn't leave us."

Grinning a terrible grin, Ronan searched through the barn until he found a hammer and some six-inch nails.

"What are you gonna do with those?" Cathy asked. "You're gonna build a cage for her? She's pretty. She'll make a nice pet."

Ronan smiled. "Just watch me."

He carried Sylvia across the barn to where several stacks of pallets stood by the wall.

After selecting one of the stacks, Ronan shoved off its top two pallets. He plumped Sylvia down on top of the remaining three, then arranged her how he wanted her, up on her hands and knees.

"Hey, Cathy, give me a hand here."

Cathy came over. "What do you want me to do?"

"Hold her up just how I've positioned her."

Cathy did so. Ronan did a final check to ensure he'd gotten Sylvia set up exactly how he wanted her, then reached into his pocket and got out one of the six-inch nails.

He spread Sylvia's right hand on the pallet wood with its palm facing downward, positioned the nail on top of it, and began hammering.

CHAPTER 24

Sylvia

Sylvia came awake to the screaming torture of torn flesh and shattered bones.

By the time she'd realized what was going on, her uncle had finished nailing her right hand to the pallet and had begun working on the left one. One slam of the hammer and her left hand was in exactly the same agony as the right one.

"STOP!" she yelled. "UNCLE RONAN, STOP! WHAT ARE YOU DOING!?"

"Hold her tight!" Ronan growled at Cathy. "I gotta do this quick now that she's awake."

Cathy held Sylvia tight. The pain in Sylvia's hands was paralyzing enough, but Cathy held her in the position she'd woken up in—kneeling and sitting on her ankles. Which she now realized was the posture of a dog sitting up.

She had no idea why this was so until, in a burst of unbelievable pain, she felt the next nail piercing the sole of her left foot and bursting through its top to bury itself in the pallet.

"NOOOOO!" she screamed. But her scream was cut off by another nail entering the same foot. And then yet another nail was rammed into her right sole.

Sylvia fainted from the agony raging through her hands and feet.

As she passed out, she heard Cathy saying:

"Alright, dad, she was the last one. I'm off to the house to have a bath and some food. You want that I should bring anything back for you?"

CHAPTER 25

Sharon & Michael & Vanni & Darrin

At the end of a long and winding lane, they pulled up to the farmhouse. A large two-story building.

"We've arrived," Darrin said.

"About damn time too," his wife agreed. "It's almost midnight. The party's missing us."

"Guys, something's wrong," Michael said. "I think we've made a wrong turn again."

"Aw, shoot," Sharon growled. "How the hell?"

"This is the right place," Darrin said. "Except Sylvia gave us wrong directions."

"GPS, baby?" This from Vanni.

"Died along with the phones at the start of the drive-in."

"Which means," said Sharon, "that this *must* be the place. I don't imagine we'll find two places in Massachusetts where the phone coverage vanishes this completely."

"Yeah, yeah," Michael agreed. "But if this is where the party's at, then where is the party?" He leaned between the seats to see the women better. "Girls, listen: I can't hear a thing."

"Not to mention that there's no cars parked anywhere," Darrin added. "Except for that old truck over there, which is likely the farmer's."

"Maybe everyone vanished along with the phone signals," Sharon joked. "This old building looks creepy enough to be that House No. 666."

"Don't you dare go *there* this close to midnight," Vanni hissed at her, pinching her thigh so she got the message.

"Let's just ask at the house," Darrin suggested. "If this is the wrong place we'll still get directions."

They got out of the car and walked over to the farmhouse, with Michael pointing out the tire tracks everywhere.

"A whole lot of people either arrived here tonight, or they left," Sharon mused as they climbed the porch steps and Darrin knocked on the front door.

The front door was opened by a slim blond teenager.

"Hello, I'm Cathy, Sylvia's cousin," the girl introduced herself. "You must be here for her birthday party."

"Yeah," Darrin agreed. "We got delayed back in Boston and—"

"Where is everyone?" Vanni interrupted him. "There's no cars here, nothing . . ."

"Oh, Sylvia and Barry had a nasty fight and she cancelled the party. Sent everyone home again."

"What?" Sharon, Vanni and Darrin all yelped at once, while Michael's mouth hung open in confusion. "But that's . . . that's crazy."

"Yeah, I know," Cathy agreed. "I'll need to explain better. But first, please, please come in and have a seat."

She stood aside to let them in. After seating everyone in the farmhouse living room, she went on with her story: "Their fight got really violent. Barry accused Sylvia of cheating on him with one of her Bain & Co. coworkers. He beat the living crap out of her—broke her nose and two ribs."

"Barry did that? But he loves her."

Cathy shrugged. "Not anymore, I don't think. He was trying to kill her—he was choking her and her face had turned purple and her tongue was sticking out and her eyes were bulging like they'd pop from her face. My dad had to knock him out before he let her go. Then he called the cops to come take him away."

"Hey, girl," Darrin said, his eyes narrowing slightly, "we got the clear impression that the phones here don't work. How'd your dad get the police?"

The blonde girl shrugged easily. "Oh, you can call from the highway. Dad drove out there. It's just here on the farm that everything's dead. Been that way for a week now."

"So everyone's gone home?" Michael asked. "Seems crazy."

Cathy nodded. "Yeah. Dad asked them to stay the night since it was so late, but lots of the wives were crying so the men took them home." She walked over to a side window and pointed outside. "You can almost see the party site from here; after the bust up, the guys who'd built the stage couldn't dismantle it fast enough. Outside of having sex, I've never seen men work that hard at night. Same with the PA guys. Both of their trucks left here barely thirty minutes ago."

"Damn," Sharon said. "You mean we drove all this way for nothing?"

"And now, we have to drive all the way back to Boston again," Vanni added with an exaggerated yawn. "For a relaxing weekend, this sure is turning out to be tiring."

"You can all stay here for the night," Cathy suggested. "It's no bother at all. We've already prepared rooms for everyone."

"Nah, we'd best be leaving," Darrin said, rising to his feet.

"Yeah," Michael agreed. "We should have called ahead on the drive over. We didn't 'cos we already knew the phones didn't work. But I guess we should've kept trying anyway. If we had we might've gotten someone who'd just left the farm to give us a heads-up on the situation here." He rose too. "Well, thanks for your time, Cathy. Is your dad home?"

"No, he's out back, working in the big barn."

"Give him our regards then." Michael gestured to Sharon and Vanni to get up.

Sharon asked Cathy, "Do you know where Sylvia was taken to?"

The girl shook her head. "I wasn't listening to the paramedics. Dad will know though. You want that I should go ask him? You'll need to wait a bit though: it's about ten minutes walk out to the old barn."

"Don't trouble yourself," Vanni said. "That's quite a distance for a young woman to walk alone at night. We'll call around our friends in the morning. Someone will know where Sylvia's hospitalized."

"Yeah, and where Barry's locked up too," Darrin added. "Son-of-a-bitch."

Michael and Darrin led the way out of the house.

"Poor Sylvia. To get beaten up on her birthday," Sharon whispered to Vanni on their way out.

"Something smells fishy here," Vanni whispered back.

"It's your fingers, from the car."

"I'm serious."

"So, what?"

"Sylvia never struck me as the cheating type."

"Do either of *us* strike you as the cheating type? Honey, there is no 'cheating type'—you do it when you do it. And against all sane

72

advice, you do it *a lot* until you get caught . . . And then you get beaten to a pulp by the guy who loves you . . . who now hates you."

With Cathy waving goodbye, they walked down to the SUV.

***

Five minutes later, Cathy was letting them back into the farmhouse again.

"Oh, no bother at all," the girl said when Darrin explained that their Audi SUV wouldn't start. "Just stay overnight and dad'll fetch you a mechanic from town in the morning."

Then, when they were all seated again, she asked, "How about something to eat? Most of the party food is still in the kitchen. There's barbeque and fries and cake and loads of drinks."

"Yeah, I'm hungry alright," Darrin said.

"Famished," Michael agreed.

Sharon nodded too.

"Yes, thank you. We're all really hungry now," Vanni said. She got up from her chair and tugged Sharon after her.

"Lead us to the kitchen," she told Cathy. "Sharon and I will give you a hand with the food."

CHAPTER 26

Sharon & Vanni

Once out of sight of their husbands, Sharon whispered in Vanni's ear, "You got me so hot on the ride over that I'm gonna need you tonight."

"Penis permitting pussy," Vanni cautioned. "Darrin's got that 'fill-your-ass' look in his eye."

"Put yours to sleep with a blowjob and I'll do the same to mine. Then we'll meet downstairs in the living room for some girl-time. I'm gonna lick your pussy to shreds."

"Ooh, I'm really gonna look forward to that. Okay, I'll try."

And then they were in the kitchen.

CHAPTER 27

Michael & Darrin

"Let's get the icebox with the beers from the SUV," Darrin told Michael once the three women had left for the kitchen. "It's about damn time I began doing some drinking of my own. You guys had all the fun in the car."

"Poor Sylvia," Michael said as they stepped outside. "That really sucks, to almost get killed on your own birthday."

"Something stinks though."

"Dude, this is a farm. Everything stinks here. Especially the sunflowers everywhere."

"I'm serious, and besides, sunflowers don't have a smell."

"They don't?"

"No they don't; something about really large flowers not needing an odor to attract pollinators. Look, man, forget the damn sunflowers. What I'm saying is, something strikes me as *wrong* here."

"What does?"

"This whole tale of Barry nearly murdering Sylvia. We both know the guy ain't the violent type."

Michael laughed. "Dude, there's no 'violent type' where guys in love are concerned. In fact, I've notice a weird correlation to this: I think the more deeply a guy loves a woman, the more passionately he's gonna beat her up when he discovers her cheating on him."

CHAPTER 28

Ben

When Ben awoke, there was a vagina in his face. He didn't at first recognize that it was a vagina, as it was still night and dark and he couldn't see a thing. He was scared, thinking some wild animal had crawled onto his head.

But then the familiar female crotch-fragrance made itself known and he relaxed a little.

"Lick me or else I'll bury you alive," a female voice said.

He realized that what had woken him was her peeling the strip of duct tape off his mouth. She'd been careful about it too, hadn't just ripped it off along with part of his mustache.

"Eat pussy or die."

Having no choice in the matter, Ben ate the anonymous vagina. The so-far unknown woman had apparently climbed down into the hole while he slept. Now she was standing over him, with her crotch pressed in his face, and her body pressed against the side of the pit, over his head.

He licked and tongued her clitoris. The vagina tasted odd, not dirty but with an exotic flavor he couldn't place; almost sugary. He didn't complain. He was in no position to complain.

She moaned, trembled, and rubbed his face all over her sex.

He kept licking.

She squirmed a lot then came.

"Lick me clean," she demanded afterward. "I don't have any tissue or wipes on me."

He did his best to comply, sucking her juices up and swallowing them down. Running his tongue up and down her thighs till she was cleansed of herself.

Only then did she step back. He saw her face by the light of her flashlight. She was young, late teens at best. She had on a short pale dress and flip-flops.

"Who are you?"

"Cathy Higgins. My dad owns this farm." She giggled. "You're trespassing on our land. We could kill you for that."

He frowned. Maybe that was a joke; but then, maybe it wasn't. Farm folk were notoriously territorial. "I'm not here by choice. Surely you can tell that."

"I feel better now," she said. "Since resurrecting, I've been horny as hell, like a bitch in heat."

Resurrecting? Not only was this lady sex-crazy, she was normal crazy too.

Ben wondered if perhaps he was still dreaming. He didn't know how long he'd slept for, but the interval hadn't helped him much. Whatever Snort had injected into him was still messing up his system. He tried to stand, but couldn't.

"Help me. I'm gonna need some assistance getting out of here."

"Not yet. Stay down there like that."

He did. She untied him.

"Hold on a minute," she said. With that, she stepped up first onto his thighs, then up onto his shoulders, then—"Hey!" he yelped as she placed a foot on his head to boost herself up—was out of the hole.

Then she was frowning down at him from the top of the hole. "Get up and stretch out your hand, and I'll pull you out."

"This might work better if you filled in the hole a bit."

The flashlight played over his face. "No. Hand."

It took all of his strength to get to his feet. Indeed, he'd not have succeeded, but Cathy grabbed his arm before he slumped back down and literally hauled him up out of the pit.

"Who dumped you in there?" she asked.

"Two close friends of mine."

"What happened to them?"

Ben remembered and shivered. He told her about the black man-creatures with the glowing eyes and embers burning inside them.

"Oh, the red-eyes got 'em." He was worried that she didn't seem worried; surprised that she wasn't surprised.

Yeah, maybe I am dreaming at that, he comforted himself. But Cathy felt remarkably solid against him. And he could still taste her on his tongue. And both the forest and the night seemed real too. He could even make out shreds of the moon through the leaf cover.

"Come with me," she said.

He felt too weak to walk, but she supported him. It wasn't too hard on her; she was clearly a very strong farm girl.

"Where are we headed?" he gasped as they staggered along. "I really can't walk too far."

"To the middle barn. My dad mustn't see you, or else you're gonna be soooo dead."

Ben understood that. No father would take lightly to the sight of his teen daughter walking somewhere in the company of a naked man in the middle of the night.

"Look," he said, "first I need to get to the car that brought me over. It's a blue Ford . . . should be parked back over there, by Route 20. My clothes and my phone are inside it."

She considered his request. "I'll get you fresh clothes."

"My phone then."

"Won't do you any good here."

She was adamant about not going back so he didn't insist.

"Cathy, earlier I heard sounds of a party. What happened to it?"

"Oh, everyone's all dead now. Even the funky DJ."

Dead? Ben felt the return of his earlier terror.

Cathy walked him past the first of three barns, from which came the soft sounds of farm animals, into the center one.

This barn, which was larger than those on either side of it, housed two tractors and three other farm vehicles. These were all parked in the building's left end. In its right end were arranged several combine harvester heads. Opposite those were stacked crates and sacks of fertilizer.

Most important for the moment though, the building also had two levels of built-in rooms: two lower rooms that seemed to be offices, and above those, another three on a platform accessed by stairs.

Cathy helped Ben up to the platform and pushed the first upstairs door open. She flicked the light switch on. "These upstairs rooms are where the farmhands sleep when they stay overnight," she explained.

The room had a bed, a chair, and a writing desk with a TV placed on it. She steered Ben towards the bed and lay him down on it.

"You'll be safe here," she told him. "Whatever you do, don't leave this barn or the red-eyes will get you too. Out there I can't guarantee your safety at all."

"Cathy, what are those red-eyed monsters?"

"My dad's business associates," she replied. "See, I was dead and my dad made a deal with Uncle Bargainer to bring me back to life by—" Then she scowled. "Nah, I mustn't bore you with that tonight. We can discuss it in the morning." She peered at him with some concern. "Have you had anything to eat?"

"No."

"Alright, I'll bring you something from the house. But first, eat *me* again."

Cathy climbed up onto the bed, knelt over Ben's face and made him perform cunnilingus on her again. Ben was too doped up to get aroused but he gave her what she wanted from him. Afterwards, she made him lick her clean again. He once more noted her sweet taste of something unfamiliar. Maybe it was a new douche flavor. Pear or peach or what?

"You're real good at eating pussy," Cathy told him happily from the bedroom door. "Okay, I'll be back in a short while with some food and drink for you. But don't worry if I delay a bit. There's guests staying the night at our house and I don't want to appear suspicious."

"Can you please turn on the TV?"

She gave him an apologetic shrug. "Sorry, doesn't work anymore. You'll just have lots of white noise. We don't get any TV reception here nowadays. No phones, no internet. Nothing. I haven't been on Facebook or Instagram since I died and came back."

"When did you die?"

"About a week ago. Look, you don't wanna know about that now. Rest and get your strength back."

She left. Ben heard a loud click as she locked the door behind her.

Since she died? She's crazy and she's a nympho and she's got me trapped in here. But, he also reminded himself, *being safe in this barn and in this warm bed is a whole lot better than being dead and buried, or even just being left in that wet pit out in the woods.*

Realizing that for the moment at least he was safe, Ben Hiller tried to make sense of what was going on.

What on earth are those horrible things she called red-eyes? Just what exactly?

CHAPTER 29

Sharon Inside

The time was about 2 a.m.

Sharon fellated the hard penis half-heartedly but with gusto. Her drunk husband groaned with pleasure. She doubted he knew her heart wasn't in it. Could men ever tell? All they cared about was the sexual performance, not the motive behind it. It was the reason prostitutes were so successful.

"Yeah, honey. Like that, just like that," Michael groaned softly as she sucked him deep into her mouth.

She let him out again, sliding her tongue delicately along the underside of his swollen manhood. He ran his fingers through her black hair. He gasped with delight.

Sharon was getting annoyed. It was taking Michael longer than normal to come. The delay was clearly due to all that wine and beer he'd drunk.

Sharon was in a hurry. She wanted to be downstairs with Vanni already. Each second longer it took Michael to ejaculate was delaying the satisfaction of her own erotic need. She wondered how Vanni was getting along with tranquilizing her own man for the night.

Hmmm, she decided a few minutes later, *this calls for my butt.*

Sharon disliked butt sex. Butt hurt. But butt it would be tonight. Men found butt irresistible. Butt was super-tight. Erections couldn't withstand butt. Butt conquered all.

"Hold on, honey," she whispered to him. "I'm gonna give you my back-door special."

She rubbed some aloe vera gel on his erection, then slid herself down on it. She was tense so it hurt more than usual. She knelt on him, lifted his hands to her breasts, clamped her aching anus even tighter around his manhood, and slowly, excruciatingly slowly, worked the penis.

It worked. He came in less than a minute.

"You're the absolute best, honey," he gasped, then fell asleep.

She lay on him till she was certain he wouldn't rouse again, then got up and wiped them both off.

It was while disposing of the soiled wipes in the plastic trash can beside the dresser, that she noticed the light in the distance.

The light was about five hundred feet away, out in the middle of the sunflower fields. It was faint like a dimming LED flashlight, purple in color, and seemed to cover an area of about forty square yards. Squinting, Sharon had the impression of dark motion within the soft glow.

What the hell is that? A UFO?

She decided she didn't care. She could ask about the light in the morning. It was most likely some government-sponsored experimental farm project.

What Sharon needed now were Vanni's firm breasts pressed against her own soft ones; Vanni's soft mouth on her own lips. Not hard muscle and penis but that juicy female tenderness she'd come to relish.

She slipped into a nightgown and slipped out of the room.

***

Reaching the stairway, Sharon felt happy, delighted with herself and with the world.

I feel so gay . . . so fucking gay. Then she giggled. *Oh, I feel gay in a non-gay way!*

She paused on the stairs for a moment to think on that.

How was it that a word could be hijacked? 'Gay' meant to be happy, not to suck dick . . . Well now it meant both being happy and men sucking dick . . . She laughed. Or maybe it meant being happy sucking dick? Or that sucking dick was the path to true happiness?

I'll have to ask Deidre Fabulous about this next time we're down at the Dark Lady gay bar in Providence. And re-watch all those old John Waters films on Netflix.

Sharon struck a pose on the stairs and pouted, as though performing before a one-woman-show audience. *Hmm, so folks . . . I suck Michael's cock a lot, does that make me gay?* She mused in amusement. *Oh and I just had butt sex with him too . . . it hurt.*

Ha ha—funny, but I'm a woman, not a guy. And, oh wow, I'm a lesbian as well now. She rolled her eyes. *Wow, modern sexuality is so damn complicated. Almost makes me wish for when my grandmom was a little girl again.*

Rather pleased with her wit, and excited by what she was off to do, she resumed her descent.

***

On reaching the bottom of the stairs, Sharon discovered that Vanni hadn't yet put Darrin to sleep. The couple were making love in the living room.

The stairwell entrance was behind the couch they were using. Darrin was out of sight, but Sharon heard him grunting hard, and then his fingers crept up and clasped tightly on Vanni's breasts. Vanni, riding her husband face-to-face, was visible from the navel up. Darrin let go of Vanni's breasts and magically became nonexistent again. The breasts bounced in celebration of freedom. Vanni's eyes were shut and she had a look of bliss on her face that Sharon was now very familiar with.

She was gasping in a low voice and making varty noises as well.

Disappointed, Sharon sat on the bottom step and waited for Vanni to open her eyes.

When, about thirty seconds later, Vanni finally noticed Sharon, her mouth formed an 'O' of surprise. But she was clearly enjoying herself with Darrin. She bent over the rear of the couch so her husband wouldn't see her facial expressions, and mouthed, "I tried to talk him out of it, but he insisted."

"You were supposed to suck *it* out of him, not talk *him* out of it!" Sharon angrily mouthed back at her.

Vanni shrugged. She looked as apologetic as a woman fast approaching orgasm could. Then Darrin grabbed her breasts again and she once more shut her eyes and resumed gasping and making varty noises.

Sharon turned to return upstairs. *Damn!* she simmered. *All that anticipation for nothing. I should have made proper love to Michael, rather than reserve myself for that slut. Vanni really doesn't seem to care as much about me as I do about her. To her, we're just fun and games!*

Midway up the stairs, Sharon stopped.

There was no way she'd ever fall asleep now.

Instead, she decided to go have a look outside and investigate the weird glow she'd noticed from her bedroom window.

She was about starting back downstairs when she realized she'd need a flashlight to navigate the sunflower field. Michael had a penlight on his key ring.

She returned to the bedroom and quietly unhooked the penlight from the key ring.

After that, she slipped on a top and some jeans, slipped on her slippers, then slipped back down to the living room and slipped past Vanni and Darrin, who were now gasping post-coital endearments to one another.

After some searching she located the farmhouse's side door and let herself out.

CHAPTER 30

Sharon Outside

The high and bright moon seemed to welcome Sharon's curiosity. Its light clearly defined the sunflower rows.

She heard a faint rattle over to her left. Slightly alarmed, she looked that way. The moonlight showed her a man in overalls walking off beyond the barns with two pails in his hand.

She calmed herself. *No, that's not a ghost. That's the old farmer, Cathy's dad. Though why he's still awake at this hour is beyond me.*

Sharon stepped in among the flowers. With no breeze moving the air, the plants' musky vegetal smell was almost overpowering.

She quickly discovered she didn't need the penlight, but she kept it on because of the danger of snakes. The moonshine revealed a clear path through the sunflower field. And her destination was also clear—the soft purple glow was barely a hundred and fifty yards away now. Through the aisles of flowers she could see it, a faintly radiant dome off a little to her right.

Very curious, she walked towards it, pushing her way through where the sunflower leaves overlapped her path. The closer she got to the glow, and the larger it got, the more bothered she became by its existence. Feeling a sudden unnatural heat in the air, she turned and stared back at the farmhouse, to reassure herself it was still there.

It remained warm. Now, the light ahead made the sunflowers throw creepy shadows around her. She clicked off the penlight. Any snakes dumb or brave enough to hang around the purple glow were welcome to bite her.

She walked closer still. When she was about thirty yards from the glow, she began making out figures. Figures moving about with unnatural silence.

I think it's time to turn back, a worried portion of her mind told her. *I got a really bad feeling about this!*

But still she went on. She wasn't just being pigheaded. She didn't feel suicidal either. She just wasn't ready to face Vanni again tonight. She expected Vanni would wait downstairs for her after she'd seen Darrin to bed. Vanni would still want to make love. But Sharon wasn't in the mood now. At the moment, Vanni was doing her best to get pregnant. Sharon did not feel like tonguing Darrin's sperm out of her vagina.

So she moved ahead.

The glow . . . what in the world is going on here?

Being a short woman, Sharon hadn't been able to see over the tops of the sunflowers. And so when she reached their edge and saw what was going on, she was completely taken by surprise.

She almost shrieked out in horror.

***

The glow let Sharon Donnelly see everything clearly, but what it revealed made no sense to her.

The purple light was coming from the depths of a huge hole. Yes, right there in the middle of the sunflower field was a massive hole in the ground. The hole looked like a sinkhole.

And . . . a ludicrously tall man in black clothes and ten-gallon hat was instructing a crew of black-but-glowing creatures to dump things into the hole.

From where she stood concealed Sharon estimated that the man had to be about twelve feet tall. He was ten yards away from her, sitting by the edge of the hole with his feet dangling into it, and even sitting down he was at least a foot taller than she was.

And if that wasn't crazy enough, she also had his companions to consider.

The creatures he was directing looked like men, but weren't. Though normal-sized, each of them was as black as coal and appeared to have a fire burning inside it. Also, their only facial features were glowing red eyes, eyes as round as vehicle headlights.

There were about twenty of the black creatures at work.

Stranger still were the things the creatures were dumping into the glowing sinkhole: to one side of the hole were four cars, two SUVs, and a truck with an open bed; and also what appeared to be a performance stage—a metal framework with a bed of long planks laid on it. Beside the stage lay several overturned loudspeakers and two barbeque grills.

Scared stiff, with one hand clamped over her mouth to stop herself screaming, Sharon watched. She'd immediately realized that here were all the vehicles and stuff from the party. The same party Cathy said had been cancelled due to a fight between the birthday girl and her boyfriend.

Oh my God! What is happening here? What's going on? Where is everyone?

She was too terrified to run away. Although she'd arrived quietly, she was certain that if she turned around now, they'd hear her and that would be that.

The monsters weren't driving the vehicles into the hole. Not at all. In each case, two of them lifted up each vehicle, one at either end of it, and carried it forward to the edge of the hole (seemingly with the ease of one moving a piece of light furniture), then threw it down and out of sight into the purple glow. The truck was similarly lifted by two of them with complete disregard for its weight, carried, and also flung away out of sight.

Once one vehicle was dumped, the tall man would gesture for them to fetch the next one.

One really inexplicable thing Sharon noticed was that the things thrown into the hole made no sound of them striking its bottom. Like the hole went down forever into the earth. Into the Abyss.

After they'd chucked down the vehicles, the black creatures threw away the party stage and PA equipment too. When they carried the planks, the wood smoked and caught fire in their grip.

Finally, the tall man climbed up from the edge of the hole and leaned over it. Sharon was amazed: upright, he seemed taller than twelve feet, maybe fifteen feet or so. She looked up, trying to see his face, but it was shrouded in shadow. The only thing she could make out about it was that it was implacably evil.

The man stared down into the hole for a few seconds, seeming to be looking for the things thrown inside it. Finally he said, "That'll do, I guess," and straightened up.

Then he called and gestured to the black creatures, who quickly gathered around him.

Clustered like this, several of the black creatures were very near to Sharon. It was now that she realized how hot they were. Pouring through the burning slits in their bodies, heat wafted off them in invisible waves that made her feel faint. She fought to remain on her feet.

She looked at their feet. Each black foot had just two fat toes, being split almost from tip to heel.

The man in black pointed to a number of the dark creatures, then to the hole. "Go!" he ordered.

Those indicated immediately leapt into the hole. He pointed again and more followed and vanished too. They leapt down without hesitation, as if they were going home.

Finally, there were only four of the horrible hot creatures left. Now the man in black pointed west. "Go!" These remaining four set off at a quick pace through the sunflowers, heading off to the west of the farmhouse.

When they were out of sight, the man clapped his hands twice. "Close!"

And just like that, the huge hole disappeared. The purple glow also instantly vanished. Where the sinkhole had existed was once more farmland sown with ripening sunflowers, gold beneath the silver moon.

"Well, there's all the evidence disposed of," the tall man said. "Ronan'll be happy about that." Then, towering above the sunflowers the way a normal-sized man towers over grass in a meadow, he too walked off to the west.

Sharon remained where she was. She waited until the tall man's footprints faded first from her ears, then from her mind.

Then, not bothering to turn her penlight on, she turned and padded back quickly between the flowers.

Shit! I need to rouse the others! We need to get away from here!

She walked for a few yards, then began running.

CHAPTER 31

Ronan

Halfway through the flower field, Ronan's foot shot out of the darkness and tripped the fleeing woman up. She went sprawling, spilling the contents of her hand into the grass.

Before she could regain her feet to continue her flight, Ronan leapt on her and hit her; a hard blow to the side of her head. She tried to scream, but her voice was gone with the dazing pain.

He rolled her over. "I've been waiting for you to come back from viewing the hole," he told her. "Hi, my name's Ronan Higgins. I'm Cathy's dad. Welcome to my farm."

Then he socked her hard on the jaw.

This time he'd knocked her out. Her body went limp and her eyes began closing.

Ronan slung the unconscious woman over his muscular shoulders and carried her off through the sunflowers towards the old barn.

He got her inside the barn and dumped her on the bloody floor.

One more for the meat pile, he thought. *I'll deal with the rest of 'em in the morning.*

For a moment he stared across at the plants in their metal tubs. They'd all begun sprouting now. And like the Bargainer had promised, they were growing fast. Damn, what strange plants they were. The more Ronan stared at the plants, the weirder they seemed to him.

No matter though. There were sixteen seeds, meaning sixteen plants.

He turned his attention to the meat pile and tried counting the bodies. Which was impossible. He'd run out of tubs. He'd had eighteen containers to begin with. Once those were used up, he'd just dumped the body parts on the floor near the two tubs he'd not used for planting. The meat pile was just that: a mess of human bits and pieces that reached as high as Ronan's waist. It stood in a lake of congealed blood—shattered bones, short lengths of arm and leg, chunks of brain, whole and halved livers, hands and feet, ropes of tangled intestines (because Ronan hadn't chopped the guts up), ears and eyeballs. A kaleidoscope of detached and dismantled flesh arranged in the morbid configurations of mass murder.

Ronan did a quick mental calculation: *Should be at least twelve bodies in there still. Yeah, I've enough meat to keep the plants healthy. And these two couples that arrived late mean another four bodies.*

He smiled. Once again he felt the unusual erotic arousal that had accompanied this whole affair. He grabbed his crotch, felt his penis hard and throbbing with excitement and need. Oh, he needed to enjoy a woman's body, and very soon at that.

Still smiling, Ronan returned his attention to the woman he'd just captured.

Quick, before she revived and made a fuss, he stripped her clothes off. Cathy was getting some well-deserved sleep and he didn't want to wait till morning to kill this one.

But then, after laying her out on the chopping block and fetching the axe, he got his first really good look at her face.

"What on earth?" he muttered to himself. "I'll be damned. It's Candy Richmond!"

He moved the unconscious woman's black hair properly away from her face and wiped some barn mud from her lips. Then he stood back and checked her appearance again. There wasn't any doubt about it.

Hell yes—it is Candy Richmond!

Excited now, Ronan flung the axe away. Hell no, he wasn't cutting this one up. Instead he stuffed a gag in her mouth, then got to work tying her up. He whistled with pleasure as he worked.

Behind him, the Bargainer's weird trees grew taller in their tubs of human meat.

CHAPTER 32

Michael, Darrin & Vanni

"Hey, guys, has either of you seen Sharon this morning?" Michael asked on descending the stairs.

It was 9 a.m. on Sunday morning. Vanni and Darrin were seated at the farmhouse dining table eating and drinking coffee. The long wooden table was piled with food: scrambled eggs and toast and delicious-smelling bacon and sausages and an assortment of fruits.

"No," Darrin replied. "We assumed she was busy chopping down your morning wood."

Vanni giggled. "We just got down here ourselves. Last I saw of her was last night after you guys went to bed, when she came back downstairs for a glass of water." She concentrated on smearing butter on a thick slice of toast.

Michael joined them at the table, but didn't sit. "Guys, I'm worried. I don't think she slept in our bed last night."

Darrin laughed. "How can you tell? You were so drunk she had to help you upstairs."

"Yeah," Vanni agreed with a grin. "Hey—sit down and have some breakfast. It's delicious. Cathy's a great cook."

Michael sat down and poured himself some coffee. "Where *is* Cathy? Maybe she's seen Sharon?"

"She went to call her dad from their old barn," Darrin replied.

Vanni swallowed her mouth of toast, then added: "The kid wasn't kidding last night when she said it was quite a way off from here. You can see the place from our bedroom window, like a giant mushroom amidst the acres of sunflowers. There's a huge pond out back there too. Looks like a huge 'L.' "

"She's been gone about twenty minutes. She's due back any minute now.

"Any luck with the car yet?"

"Nah, son-of-a-bitch machine still won't start. Even the inside lights won't turn on. It's like some robot hunter shot the engine dead in the concrete jungle."

Cathy walked in five minutes later, accompanied by Ronan.

"Morning, everyone," Ronan greeted cheerily. "Welcome to the Higgins Farm. Sorry I couldn't be here last night to welcome you personally, but I had all this mutton to cure out in the barn and it took forever to get it set up properly; so I ended up snoozing out there." He smiled from face to face. "Now, Cathy tells me you're having some trouble with your SUV. I can easily drive into Chester for a mechanic. No bother at all."

"Thanks, sir," Darrin said. "I'm Darrin and this is my wife Vanni, and this is Michael and—"

"Have you seen my wife anywhere?" Michael asked. "I haven't seen her this morning. She's petite with long black hair and I think was wearing jeans and a tee shirt."

He'd addressed his question to Ronan. But Ronan didn't reply. Ronan was staring at Vanni. Really staring at her.

"Hey," he said after a while. "I know you. You're that porno actress Mandy Paris!"

Vanni stiffened. Cathy's eyes widened in surprise. Michael and Darrin, however, burst out laughing. Darrin's explosion of laugher was so intense that his mouthful of coffee went down the wrong way and he wound up coughing.

Vanni glared at the two men. Michael was laughing so much that he had tears in his eyes.

She turned her attention back to Ronan. "I'm not a porno actress," she said coldly. "I'm his wife."

"But . . . but . . ." Ronan looked really confused.

"No 'buts' about it," Vanni said firmly, her voice still frosty. She pointed to her husband. "The only dick I suck for a living belongs to this dick here."

"But you must be Mandy—" Ronan went on.

"Hey, dad, stop it!" Cathy interrupted him. "You're embarrassing her!"

Ronan shrugged and fell silent.

Vanni glared at Darrin, who'd just managed to get his mirth under control. "I don't see what you two are laughing at. He's implying I'm a slut and you're finding it funny?"

"Sir," Darrin addressed Ronan, "I'll humbly admit that my wife is super-hot, but mistaking her for a porno actress is a bit much, don't you think?"

Ronan nodded. "Then she's really not the one? I really thought . . ."

"I'm not your porno girl," Vanni said flatly, looking like she'd start crying. "What on earth gave you that impression?"

"Dad, stop it!" Cathy pleaded. "Let it go, for God's sake!"

Ronan raised his hands apologetically.

"I'm sorry, Vanni," he said. "I don't mean any offence. It's just rare to see two people who look so alike. You look so much like Mandy Paris, you could be two peas in a pod."

Darrin looked to be about to start laughing again, until Vanni cut him with a scathing look. "But I'm not."

"Yes, yes, of course not. You've convinced me of that. Like I said, I apologize. I didn't mean to upset you."

There was an awkward silence for a few moments, then Michael, who also seemed on the verge of bursting into laughter again, asked: "Yes, I was asking if you've seen my wife around the farm buildings."

Ronan's brow creased up in thought for a while. "Shortish and slim, with long black hair? Wearing jeans and a short-sleeved blue top?"

"Yes, that's her alright. Did you see her, sir?"

Ronan nodded. "Yes, I did. Around six-thirty I came back to the third barn—that's the one where we occasionally lock in the sheep when there's gonna be a rainstorm—and I saw her. Behind the barn, near the dog kennels, there's a gap in the woods through which you can see the road that leads out from here, and I saw her walking down the road." He shrugged. "I dunno, maybe she went to make a phone call by Route 20. You know how there's no phone signal around the house anymore."

"Thanks," Michael said. "That's a relief. We'll go find her after this great breakfast which Cathy so nicely provided."

"Yeah," Ronan said, pulling Cathy close and hugging her. "My little girl's a really useful girl when she wants to be." Avoiding looking at

Vanni now, he sat down with them and helped himself to a slice of toast and some scrambled eggs. Cathy sat also but didn't eat.

"Eat, girl," Ronan encouraged her. "We've a lot of work to get through today."

The girl shook her blonde head. "I ain't hungry, dad. I'm only sitting here to ensure you don't start picking on Ms. Vanni again."

They all laughed at that.

"Crazy how last night's party broke up, ain't it?" Vanni asked cautiously after a while.

Ronan nodded and swallowed. "Craziest thing I ever saw in all my life. I ain't never seen a man go for a woman like that before." He shook his head. "Damn. You could see it written in his eyes that he was going to murder her."

"Mike and I were discussing that last night," Darrin said. "We honestly never suspected Barry was that sort of a person . . ."

CHAPTER 33

Michael & Darrin

Once breakfast was over, Michael and Darrin headed down the road to search for Sharon. Both men had their cellphones with them.

Had Michael taken the time to look through his wife's handbag before setting out, he'd have seen that she'd not taken her phone with her.

But now both men assumed Sharon had either lain down somewhere and fallen asleep, or was engaged in a long and engrossing phone conversation, possibly with Michael's sister Ann, and had lost track of time.

It was a warm, wettish morning. As with the farmhouse yard, parts of the farm road were still muddy from yesterday afternoon's rain.

Both men thought the atmosphere felt odd, but it was Darrin who finally mentioned it.

"This place feels weird," he said.

"I feel it too," Michael agreed. "Something's wrong with this farm."

"Yeah, but what?"

"I think it's just all these damn sunflowers everywhere. Give me cornfields any day."

They'd reached the start of the forest. Ahead, the road bent sharply right; the rest of it was out of sight amongst the trees.

"You think that's all?" Darrin asked.

"For the moment I do. I won't be sure until we've found Sharon."

"Then we gotta wait for Ronan to wake up again."

Michael shrugged. "At least we're not stranded out in the middle of nowhere. That'd be a total drag. Here we can at least relax till help arrives."

***

During breakfast, Ronan had fallen asleep at his place at the table. Cathy had woken him up and seen him up to bed.

"He's like that," she'd apologized afterward. "Works too much. I don't think he actually slept at all last night."

Michael had asked Cathy for the keys to her father's pickup truck, so he and Darrin could make the drive into Chester instead and save Ronan the bother.

Cathy had been unable to find the keys. So they would have to wait for Ronan to wake up again.

***

Michael and Darrin walked in silence for a while. Down the makeshift country road, with wet earth sticking to their shoes. Each constantly checked their phones for a signal. So far there was nothing.

Then Darrin laughed out loud.

"Dude?" Michael asked, then began laughing himself.

"Man, did you see the look on Vanni's face when Ronan asked her that question? It was absolutely priceless!"

Both men stopped walking, grabbed their bellies and laughed and laughed and laughed. Michael laughed so much that he staggered off the road and leaned against a tree till he got control of himself.

Then, tears streaming down his face, he asked Darrin: "Dude, do you think our wives have the slightest idea that we know they're fucking each other?"

"Didn't you see the look on Vanni's face? They don't suspect a damn thing!"

This gave way to a whole lot more laughter.

CHAPTER 34

Cumwithcandyandmandy.com

A month and a half ago Michael Donnelly had driven back from the office midmorning to pick up a property brief he'd forgotten at home.

Sharon hadn't been home at the time, so he'd let himself in the front door. He'd almost immediately found the folder he was after, but then, about to leave for work again, he'd wondered where his wife was. Calling her phone just went to voicemail.

Then it had occurred to Michael that Sharon might be over at Vanni's place. Once she'd dropped Davey off at kindergarten, she might have gotten bored being by herself and gone over there for some chat and coffee.

Michael walked over between the houses. He didn't go by the front door. Both families had long ago taken to visiting each other via their kitchen doors, an easy walk across the two adjacent lawns.

So Michael walked over there. Even before reaching the Warren's kitchen he could hear noises. Odd yet familiar noises that made him slow the tread of his feet.

He didn't knock on the kitchen door. Instead, he peeked in the window to see what was going on in there.

Then, shocked, he remained there watching.

Vanni was up on the kitchen island with her legs parted. Sharon—his own darling Sharon—was licking Vanni between the legs. Vanni's eyes were shut, her blonde hair was scattered. She was clutching a fistful of Sharon's black hair and with it was urging the smaller woman to greater sexual exertion.

Confident that no one else was around, they weren't being quiet.

"You're getting better at eating pussy, woman," Vanni moaned. "A little more practice and you'll be almost as good as Darrin is."

Sharon's response was to lick two fingers to wetness and thrust them between Vanni's legs, which instantly upped her gasping and moaning. Vanni's small breasts shone with a delicate sheen of sweat.

I married a closet lesbian? Michael was confused. Sharon had never shown signs of being sexually attracted to women.

Then Michael felt betrayed and angry. Enraged. He would rush in there and beat the crap out of these two cheating jezebels. No, better still, he'd grab a knife and murder them . . . no, he'd find Darrin's gun and shoot them both dead. They didn't deserve better than death!

But then his confusion returned. He stood there, aroused by the sight, feeling let down, and at the same time feeling strangely guilty, as if he was viewing something he shouldn't be.

Vanni had a loud, loud orgasm, then Sharon switched places with her on the kitchen island and spread her legs too.

For two minutes, Michael watched his wife squirming and moaning to another woman's caresses. Then, feeling a strange calm settle over him, he quietly backed away.

While he made his retreat, Sharon was gasping, "Yeah, lick my butt, you suburban slut!"

They didn't even notice I was there, Michael thought to himself as he drove off.

***

"Lick my butt, you suburban slut? Now that's nasty. That's porn star nasty," Darrin said that evening when Michael related to him what he'd seen.

"The bitches didn't even notice I was there," Michael rounded up his angry tale.

He and Darrin had gone out for drinks, to a quiet uptown bar where they could talk in private.

At first Darrin had been surprised to hear what was going on. But then he'd smiled coldly. Darrin Warren wasn't by nature a nasty man, but he could be ruthless when provoked. "So that's why she's been treating me so nicely these past two months."

"Huh?"

"I mean Vanni. She's been all sweetness and cream to me, gives me head even before I suggest it, is ready to make love whenever I want."

"I don't get you."

Darrin waved his whiskey in an expansive gesture. "I mean, my wife is exhibiting a guilt complex. She's having sex with me all the time so I don't suspect she's having sex behind my back too." He grinned at Michael. "Think, dude—how has Sharon been treating *you* in the sack?"

Michael's face creased up. "Hmmm, now you mention it . . . yeah, she's more horny for it nowadays too. But . . . but I thought that's just 'cos we're trying to make a second baby."

"Yeah, the baby was my original conclusion too."

They drank in silence for a while, eyeing the waitresses in their short skirts. Then Darrin asked Michael, "So what about it? What do you plan on doing now that you know?"

Michael scowled. "We're . . . I'm getting a divorce," he said. "How the hell can she . . . can they . . . ?"

Darrin shrugged. "What about your kid? Divorce her and she'll get your little boy. Mothers always have preference where young children are concerned."

"Shit. I don't wanna lose Davey."

"I know you don't. Look, let's do this my way. Personally, I don't seen any point in divorcing Vanni. Who's to say her replacement won't be organizing gangbangs while I'm at work?"

"You're taking this really cool. Me, I'm traumatized."

"That's 'cos you're thinking like a woman—like one of *them*. Calm down and use your *man*-brain for a moment. You don't need to get a divorce. The way I see it, this presents an opportunity for us. A great opportunity. We're gonna pimp them."

"I don't follow you."

"Oh, you will. You're gonna love what I've got in mind."

"Man, it hurts. I feel like I've been stabbed in the heart."

"You mean stabbed in the dick. You're just upset that Sharon's moaning to a woman. You're worried that Vanni's better than you in bed."

"And you aren't?"

Darrin smiled his cold smile again, sipped his whiskey and laughed. "Me? I'm a sexual philosopher."

"I don't follow you."

"Women are like books," he said.

"I still don't follow you."

"View it this way: why buy just one, when there's a whole library of them from which you can borrow, read, and return afterwards?"

"Man, you're so cold."

Darrin grinned. "And your dad raised the last boy scout. Think, consider the opportunity this betrayal presents. Are you really gonna tell me that you don't wanna bang that cute secretary of yours?"

An image of Jackie Kemper's tight rump came to Michael's mind. The pretty girl had a habit of wearing very formfitting outfits and finding all kinds of excuses to bend over whenever Michael summoned her into his office. "Well . . . uh . . ."

"Well, now you can do so without any scruples." Darrin raised a cautionary finger. "So long . . . so long as you don't knock her up. Even to a cheating woman that's unforgivable. If you pregger Miss Kemper up, Sharon can kill you and the courts will still grant her custody of your kid."

"But . . . another secretary? Darrin, Sharon used to be my secretary and look what's happened. How do I know this one won't turn out worse?"

"Simple, because you ain't gonna marry the woman. She'll just be pleasure on the side. Our wives will be having their fun, and you and me? We'll be having ours right along with them. Mike baby, we'll be having our cake *and* eating it—we still get to enjoy our wives too."

"Alright, alright," Michael finally agreed, largely convinced by images of Jackie Kemper's buttocks bouncing up and down on his penis in the first motel room he could book them into. Out of town, of course. "But I still wanna pay Sharon back in some way for breaking my ego. What did you mean when you said we're gonna pimp them?"

Darrin grinned a wolf's grin. "Simple. Our wives wanna be lesbian sluts? Well, we're gonna make them *famous* lesbian sluts."

***

And that had been the origin of cumwithcandyandmandy.com

What Michael and Darrin had done was to wire up Darrin's house with high definition video cameras and upload the filmed content to a website they'd set up.

To set the house up, Darrin had enlisted the help of a surveillance-savvy friend of his named Jojo Kim. Jojo was an eccentric half Korean, half American movie producer, diva, and occasional hacker. She also managed her younger sisters' band, Kimchi Chocolate Stereo.

Jojo had a weird sexual fetish which Darrin agreed to help her fulfil if she bugged his house for him.

That deal made, the next weekend both couples flew south to Las Vegas for some fun and gambling, Darrin having already given Jojo a set of his house keys.

By the time they returned home, everything was ready.

Jojo Kim had installed sixteen tiny and unnoticeable HD video cameras in the house. It didn't matter where Sharon and Vanni did it, their husbands would have their pretty vaginas and sexy bodies on film.

The software that ran the cameras was originally the property of one Uncle Sam, aka the US government. It was cutting-edge technology designed to record terrorist conversations. Jojo Kim had stolen the software and its passwords from her CIA-spy father. After some minor reverse engineering, the filched software was perfectly adapted to filming porn. Its main advantage was its 'auto face-track' feature, which enabled it to turn its multiple cameras on and of as the visual target moved around within its location, thus reducing the amount of footage saved to disk. Applied to porn, what this meant was automatic recording of a sex scene as one continuous video stream, but with continual switching of camera angles to capture the most important moments.

Michael and Darrin had already registered the website cumwithcandyandmandy.com.

A portable server uploaded everything the HD cameras recorded to cloud storage for the husbands to access at their leisure. Each Friday night both men sat down to review the week's footage. They were usually very impressed with what their wives had gotten up to sexually. Sharon, in particular, was always coming up with new cosplay outfits and routines. Almost as if she knew she was being filmed. But of course, she didn't. She also kept coming up with new sex toys for herself and Vanni to try out. Once she'd brought over a double dildo so large that both men winced when they saw their wives fitting it into themselves.

"Where the hell does she buy those things from?" Darrin had asked Michael.

"Where the hell in our house does she hide them?" Michael had asked Darrin.

Each Friday night Michael and Darrin would select the best footage, edit and tag it, add some music and credits, and upload it to the website.

The husbands weren't really out to embarrass their wives, so they'd given them pseudonyms. Sharon was Candy Richmond and Vanni was Mandy Paris.

What the husbands had initially intended was just to have some payback laughs at their wives' expense. And also, as Darrin once pointed out, "It provides us with a video record of their infidelity. Just in case. You never know."

They honestly hadn't expected anyone to really show an interest in the website. After all, the internet was chock-full of housewife porn.

But people *did* show an interest in cumwithcandyandmandy.com. By two weeks after its launch, the porn site already had a large and enthusiastic following.

Meanwhile, Michael began dating Miss Kemper, and Darrin had affairs with two women.

And then, things snowballed. Before Michael and Darrin realized it, they were knee-deep in rabid subscribers.

Something about 'Candy' and 'Mandy'—actually it was the women's non-performance innocence while having sex, since they had no idea they were being filmed—was attracting men like flies to sugar. And Sharon's ceaseless experimentation with toys and sex positions ensured the videos never got stale or boring.

Michael and Darrin had another emergency discussion over drinks:

"If the girls find out, they're gonna kill us," Darrin said wearily.

"And Sharon'll still get custody of Davey afterwards," Michael agreed morosely.

"I never thought it could possibly get this big."

"We gotta stop this."

"Yeah, but it's making us loads of easy money. The subscribers can't get enough of Candy and Mandy. Now they even want live webcam shows."

"C'mon, man, we can still reel this in. But once we ink that DVD deal with Titaholics Anonymous there's no going back anymore."

"But Titaholics? Dude, that's the porno big time. We'll really be raking the money in then. They want three DVDs worth of stuff. And they'll release it in Europe too."

"Have you considered what'll happen if we accidentally win an AVN award?"

"Yeah, your wife and my wife are gonna kill me and you. Dude, I'm gonna start leaving my Sig P220 in the office."

"You don't care, do you, man?"

"Screw 'em. Their fault. And as we worry here, they're *still* screwing around on us. Besides, what have they got to complain about anyway? We've made them famous!"

"Man, but we gotta do something."

"Yeah, we gotta make more money off of this!"

"Dude, let's just go home and bang the two horny bitches. This problem will still be here in the morning."

"Yeah, man; it will."

It was while they were pondering on whether or not to shut down the Candy and Mandy website before their wives found out about it, that Sylvia Stewart's birthday party came up.

And so here they were now.

CHAPTER 35

Cathy & Vanni

"I'm sorry about dad picking on you back there," Cathy said, while following Vanni back inside the house after Michael and Darrin had vanished from sight around the first bend in the road. "Sometimes he just gets like that."

Vanni shrugged. "Oh, it's alright. In fact, in a way it's rather flattering. What woman doesn't want to be mistaken for a porn star? It means you're hot as fire." She laughed. "It was just so unexpected, that's all." She stared back out the door for a moment, shaking her head. "I can't believe those two lunkheads found it so hilarious."

"They're men," Cathy said understandingly as they moved to sit at the dining table again. "I always find guys funny. You know? Like they're a joke life is playing on us women."

Vanni poured herself a final cup of coffee. "Is there a chance that Sharon actually walked off towards your old, distant barn? I mean, if she like, returned from the highway while we were all in here and didn't feel like joining us for breakfast? Or, if maybe on her way back she took that shortcut near the barns that your father mentioned."

Cathy looked at her in surprise. "You know, I hadn't considered that possibility. Hmmm, we'd better walk over there and have a look." Then she shook her head. "No—I'll go. Best that you wait here. If we both visit the barn and your husbands return while we're gone, they'll start wondering what's happened to you instead of Ms. Sharon. And if in the meantime Ms. Sharon returns without them, she's gonna wonder too where everyone's vanished to."

Vanni sipped her coffee. "Yeah, that makes sense. Fine then. You go, I'll stay here."

Cathy nodded. "Alright, just give me a few minutes and I'll hurry out there."

Once Cathy had left the house, Vanni, coffee mug in hand, walked outside and stood on the front porch regarding the morning. The weather was nice, but she felt something odd in the atmosphere, something that bristled with bad intent; as though today were an evil monster that would consume them all.

She shivered.

Having no explanation for the sudden unease she felt, Vanni sat down on the porch steps to await everyone's return.

CHAPTER 36

Michael & Darrin

"Any signal yet, man?"

"None. Dude, this is getting tedious."

They were halfway along the access road now. It was a meandering route that in the light of day and on foot seemed a whole lot longer than it had while motoring up it the previous night. The bends in the road and the trees all around created an illusion in the walkers that they weren't moving at all.

Darrin held his phone up. "Damn, still nothing." He slipped the phone into his pocket. "Doesn't matter, I guess. We're sure to find Sharon at the turnoff anyway."

"You know," Michael said. "This farmer Ronan here recognizing Vanni makes me a bit bothered."

"You shouldn't be."

"But we do need to consider this. The more popular our wives become online, the more it's gonna keep happening. They'll be recognized left, right, and center. It'll take just one more person saying something similar—for instance, a guy they meet at the mall—and then . . ."

Darrin laughed. "Okay, so they find out. What else can possibly happen other than them threatening divorce?"

"Quite a frigging lot," Michael replied nervously. "Worse case scenario? Just imagine this: The girls find out what we did and divorce us. But then, we now discover that we've gotten them both pregnant in the interim, so now I'll have two kids and you'll have one and . . ."

Darrin stopped laughing. "And you, my friend, have got an overly active imagination. It's *their* damn fault! They're still cheating on us with each other!"

Michael went on like he'd not heard him: "And then, just to spite us, after the divorces they remain together as a lesbian couple, and also remain in the porno industry, going on to become world-famous porn stars of the Jenna Jameson status of celebrity, and we their ex-husbands have to pay child support and seek their permission to visit our kids. And now we *have to* watch them doing their lesbian kissing and fondling routine. Everyone we know will mock us. We'll be considered world-famous losers."

"Man, you worry a whole damn lot. You know that?" Darrin threw up his hands in exasperation. "Alright, you win. Once we get back to Boston, we'll shut down the website. How's that? Heck, I can't believe all the money we're gonna lose 'cos you're scared of . . . of . . . of . . . HOLY SHIT!"

He'd cussed because, stepping towards them around the next bend in the road was the tallest man either of them had ever seen. The man was at least eight feet tall and was dressed completely in black leather clothes, including a black ten-gallon hat. He was thin too. His face was lined with age—like he was a billion years old—despite which a horrifying vitality emanated from his coal black eyes.

"Am I seeing this guy for real?" Michael whispered.

"That's what I'm asking myself," Darrin replied. "But we gotta be. Neither of us has smoked any of that hash you brought along."

"Man, he looks like that guy in *Machete*. What's his name again? The Mexican actor?"

"Who? Oh, you mean Danny Trejo. No, he doesn't. Trejo's got a mustache."

"Yes he does. This guy looks the way Trejo would look if he *didn't* have a mustache. No no no—he looks the way Trejo's great-great-great-grandfather would look if he were still alive and didn't have a mustache."

"Stop talking shit, man."

"I can't help it. Just look at this guy. He's a freak of nature."

They would both have loved to turn and run for their lives, but the impossibly tall man was heading straight for them. He stopped a few paces away and hailed them. A cold smile creased his thin lips, lips the texture of leather left out in the Mojave Desert.

"Hi, friends, I'm the Bargainer," he said in a rasping baritone. He gestured up at the sky. "This *is* such a wonderful morning, ain't it? Yeah, one of God's finest."

The Bargainer?

Michael got over his fear first. Staring up at the giant, he asked, "Good morning to you too, sir. Hey, you haven't by any chance seen my wife this morning, have you? She's smallish, has long black hair and—"

"—Was wearing blue jeans and a tee shirt and was trying for a phone signal down by the junction," the Bargainer finished for him. "Yeah, sure, I've seen her."

"That's a relief," Darrin said, finally finding his own voice. "Is she still down there now?"

The giant shook his head. "Nah, she's gone."

The faintest shiver of fear ran through Michael. "Gone where?"

The Bargainer leaned over so that their three heads were close together. The two husbands now felt a cold, almost reptilian sense of repulsion about him, like they were standing next to a poisonous snake.

"No need to get worried," the Bargainer said. "What I meant is, she got a signal down there and spoke awhile with someone. Then she headed back towards the farm."

"But, she isn't there," Darrin said.

"That's 'cos she stepped off the road just a short while later." The thin giant pointed over their heads, into the forest on their right. "She went that way—I think she was headed for those three barns. Well, something over there attracted her attention for sure."

Michael and Darrin followed his long fingers with their eyes.

"If you head over there you're sure to find her," the man said behind them. "Yeah."

"Hey, my man, thanks."

"Don't mention it, friends."

But when they'd both turned around again, the giant had vanished. He was gone without a trace. They couldn't see him in the distance; nor did they hear any rustling amidst the trees on the other side of the road that would suggest he'd stepped off the road into the forest. It was as if they'd been holding a conversation with the wind.

"You sure you didn't mix pot with that pot of coffee?" Michael asked after a pregnant pause.

Darrin shook his head. "Oh, he was here alright. See, those are his footprints in the mud leading back down the road. But . . . but . . . but . . ."

Michael knew what Darrin's 'but' was: coming up the road towards them, they could see the clear impressions of a set of enormous size 40 feet. But beyond the last two muddy footprints, which stopped right beside them, there weren't any others; neither proceeding farther along the dirt road nor stepping aside into the forest . . . as if . . .

As if the man who'd called himself 'the Bargainer' had simply faded into the air after conversing with them.

"Man, I'm beginning to feel very spooked," Michael said nervously. He ran his fingers through his brown hair. He did look like he'd just seen a ghost. He thought he had too.

"Me too," Darrin agreed with a shiver. He forced his gaze away from the truncated trail of tracks, then stared his best friend cold in the eyes. "Dude, let's go find your wife. I'm beginning to think we've more to worry about here than just being divorced by our closet lesbians."

CHAPTER 37

Ronan & Sharon

Unknown even to Cathy, Ronan was currently out in the distant barn.

While Vanni and his daughter had been escorting the two husbands over to the start of the farmhouse road, Ronan had slipped out the back door and made his way through the sunflower fields to the large barn.

If the two men came out this way he would claim he'd forgotten his truck keys out here and come to fetch them.

They'd likely be searching for the missing wife for most of the morning.

Enough time.

Ronan stared across at the 'missing' woman. She'd revived now and was looking confused. Confused and terrified by the sights around her.

Also revived was his niece Sylvia, who, with her hands and feet nailed firmly to that top pallet, just looked to be in agony.

Before paying any further attention to his captives, Ronan took a good look at the plants he was growing. Wow, they were really sprouting fast now. As he'd been warned to, except during feeding times he stood a cautious distance away from the tubs. The damn things were growing rapidly, as though human flesh were the Devil's fertilizer.

Each plant was now five feet tall. The main visible oddities about them were their tentacles. They had no branches or leaves, just a spread of six or seven black tentacles each that began about three feet up their equally black trunks. The lower parts of their trunks also housed a large humanish mouth filled with long and pointed yellow teeth. Each demon-plant had at least one mouth; several had up to three of them. The plants fed by picking up the human flesh with their tentacles. The mouths chewed and dripped blood from reddened lips.

Five of the plants had eaten up most of the flesh piled around them. In these five cases, one could see their roots at the bottom of their metal tubs. Their roots were human arms and hands; all black as night, their palms and fingernails inclusive. Ronan shivered whenever he looked at those roots. They seemed completely unnatural to him.

Using a shovel with a long handle, Ronan refilled the emptied tubs from the corpse-meat pile. The stink of blood and death was thick in the barn air. Whenever Ronan got too close to the plants, they stretched their tentacles towards him, trying to catch him for additional breakfast.

He worked in silence for a while, occupying his mind by regarding the barn's other four tenants.

The four remaining red-eyes stood motionless in the corner behind Sylvia. The demon creatures were like statues carved from anthracite; idols in a shrine dedicated to the worship of Fire—the most feared element of all. Cooped in as they now were, Ronan felt their temperature from where he stood. The red-eyes' heat felt as though it were their thoughts and voices. The air trembled over the hellish creatures' crack-riddled bodies. Their eyes glowed like the mouths of erupting volcanos. They themselves seemed filled with molten lava, its glow pulsing eternally unabated within.

Their heat made the barn hot. Ronan wished he could phone the farmhouse and ask Cathy to bring him a drink of water.

But calling anywhere was out of the question. The Bargainer had supernaturally shut down all telecommunication over the Higgins Farm until 'the project' was completed. Even the radio Ronan had here for company didn't work now.

Ronan hadn't yet questioned the Bargainer as to what the red-eyes actually were, but in his gut of guts they struck him as being mindless carved blocks of stone animated by an evil power.

And, he now understood, evil was relative. Evil had relatives too. He, Ronan Higgins, was now directly related to Evil; as much as if they were products of the same womb.

The Bargainer had left these four red-eyes as 'insurance.' "In case you have any trouble while I'm not around," he'd explained. "Just tell them what you want them to do and they'll do it."

Then, to further 'energize' Ronan, he'd given the farmer another drink of demon elixir.

Ronan did feel energized; but the drink was having some obvious side effects on him too; one of which was his burgeoning libido. And, a short while ago he'd also felt two hard inexplicable bumps on his forehead.

Ronan finished shoveling meat for the black plants. Once again his penis had gotten stiff while he'd been working. He'd lost count of how many erections he'd had since yesterday. His balls hurt something awful. He needed a woman and right now.

Reaching a decision, he strode over to the 'missing' wife—the one who looked like Candy Richmond. 'Candy' was sitting against the gore-splattered workbench where he'd left her, her legs bound, her arms also tied behind her. Her hair and clothes were flecked with blood clots and scraps of flesh and skin that had dropped on her from the workbench

She trembled at his approach, shrinking back from him as if he was Satan incarnate, attempting to force her small body through the stone wall.

He reached down and yanked the gag from her mouth.

He smiled at her. "Hi, Candy."

He was surprised by her reaction. Just the same as when he'd greeted Mandy Paris in the farmhouse (he was certain she really was the one), Candy too appeared genuinely confused by his greeting.

"Who's Candy?" she asked tentatively.

"Why, *you're* Candy, of course. Candy Richmond. Don't you dare try to deceive me like Mandy just did. I know you're Candy Richmond, the porno actress."

Now she really looked surprised.

But Ronan was growing impatient; he needed his erection taken care of. It couldn't be merely coincidence that they'd both appeared together in his house on the same day. So what silly game did they imagine they were playing on his intelligence? First that one, and now this one? "Hey, quit with the dumb act," he growled at her. "I'd know you from a mile off. You're one of my favorite porno actresses. I'm a subscriber to your website, cumwithcandyandmandy.com."

Now her response really surprised him:

"I'M NOT A GODDAMN PORNO ACTRESS, YOU ASSHOLE!" she screeched, so loud that Ronan thought his ears would burst from the noise. "AND I'M NOT CANDY WHAT-THE-FUCK RICHMOND! MY NAME IS SHARON DONNELLY! I'M A GODDAMN RESPECTABLE SUBURBAN HOMEMAKER WITH A RICH HUSBAND AND A FIVE-YEAR-OLD SON WHO'S CURRENTLY SPENDING THE WEEKEND WITH MY SISTER-IN-LAW BECAUSE WE CAME HERE TO ATTEND YOUR GODDAMN NIECE'S BIRTHDAY PARTY!"

Ronan got used to her voice. It wasn't too strident. It was actually quite pleasant once one adjusted to the volume. His daughter Cathy sounded much worse when she didn't get her way and threw a tantrum. And besides, the barn was too far off for anyone to hear Candy screaming anyway.

Ronan unzipped his denim pants and pulled out his erection. He regarded it curiously as he held it in his hand. This was another side effect of that drink the Bargainer had given him: his penis had both gotten twice as large as previously and was now mottled pink and blue, like a piebald horse dick that God Almighty hadn't had enough black ink on hand to finish coloring. The blue on his phallus could have come from his jeans—it was the same tint. And it wasn't just his penis either: the skin on Ronan's belly and thighs was similarly discolored now. It didn't hurt or anything like that, but it sure looked odd to him.

It looked odd to Candy too. But maybe it wasn't just the erection's unusual color that had her fazed. He'd never seen a woman's eyes widen as much as hers did when she saw the size of his penis.

He pointed the massive pink and blue erection at 'Candy.' "Alright, baby, which will it be: A blowjob or your life?"

She began screaming again: "NO, NO, NO! I WILL NOT SUCK YOUR HORRIBLE COCK, YOU PSYCHOTIC JERKOFF!"

"Hey, hey—stop acting the prude, bitch. You're a porno actress."

"WHAT THE HELL IS WRONG WITH YOU, YOU INSANE BASTARD!? I'M *NOT* A PORNO ACTRESS! I'M SHARON DONNELLY—SHARON DONNELLY! I'M A MARRIED WOMAN! I'M A RESPECTABLE HOUSEWIFE! I'M HERE WITH MY HUSBAND AND I REALLY LOVE HIM AND I DON'T SLUT AROUND FOR PERVERTS LIKE YOU TO JERK OFF TO!"

He found it weird: she seemed genuinely angry. So angry that she was disregarding the danger she was in.

Ronan frowned coldly at the irate woman. He shook his foot-long piebald erection threateningly at her. "Alright, so you're Sharon Donnelly. So frigging what? So no blowjob then? Not even to save your respectable suburban life?"

She smirked at him, her disgust exceeded only by her pity. When she spoke now, her voice was gentle and scornful: "Only in Hell, buster, and even there the Devil would have to force my mouth open to admit your stinking penis!"

"I'll kill you if you don't." He moved his penis close to her mouth and grabbed her jaw. She bit his hand. He jerked back swearing.

"Okay, you asked for this!"

"Go jump in the Boston harbor, asshole," Sharon spat at Ronan. She got loud again: "I WOULDN'T SUCK YOUR NAUSEATING COCK IF THE SURVIVAL OF ALL LIFE ON EARTH DEPENDED ON IT! NOT EVEN IF TOUCHING IT WOULD TURN THIS PLANET INTO A PARADISE!"

"Well, if you won't suck my dick, what goddamn use are you?" Ronan asked her.

"SCREW YOU! THE POLICE ARE GONNA GET YOU FOR THIS! YOU'LL ROT IN JAIL FOR—!"

That was the last thing Sharon Donnelly ever said. Her eyes gaped in surprise when the descending axe split her head completely in two. She'd not noticed Ronan pick the axe up off the workbench.

The left half of her head remained in place; the right half slid down the left half, then off of her neck and shoulders, in a mess of blood and brains and shattered bone and teeth.

Ronan stared at the dead woman for a while. *Damn, what a waste.*

Her complete denial of her ever filming any porn puzzled him. He knew for sure that she was Candy Richmond.

Well, maybe not. Ronan doubted that a bona fide porno actress would be so dumb as to lose her life over a goddamn blowjob. Dying over a blowjob?

He spat down on her corpse. *Retard bitch. Like maybe she thought I was bluffing. Now I'm gonna chop you up too and let the plants dispose of the evidence. Great thing that they eat up all the bones as well.*

The problem was, killing Candy/Sharon had just made Ronan's penis harder.

Seeing all the fresh red blood spilling from her corpse and settling over the previously congealed red mess on the barn floor was getting him more and more sexually excited.

This is getting to be quite a headache, he mused.

He stared across the barn, wondering whether to dispatch the red-eyes to fetch him the other woman—the hot blonde who also claimed not to be the porno actress Mandy Paris. But then his gaze alighted on his niece Sylvia.

Sylvia was staring at Ronan and shivering. If she'd been frightened before by all the pain she was in, and also the insane things her uncle was growing (things that were currently eating her closest, most dear friends), now she was utterly terrified. She'd not stopped shaking since seeing Ronan chop Sharon's head in two as deftly as if it was wood he was splitting. And now, as he walked over to her with the bloodstained axe in hand, she saw two red protrusions on his forehead, one on each side.

Horns, she thought in additional terror, *he's growing horns!*

Ronan reached her, penis sticking out of his fly like a gun barrel.

"Alright, niece," he said gruffly. "I'm gonna ask you the same question as I asked her—a blowjob or your life?"

Even through the overwhelming pain of her hands and feet that were nailed to the pallet, Sylvia managed to summon up some righteous indignation: "But you can't! You *can't* have sex with me! You're my uncle, for goodness' sake. Mom's brother!"

Ronan nodded. "Yeah, that's right. I am." Then he pointed down at his throbbing penis. "But does this look like it understands family relationships?" His expression turned evil. "Now listen up. Because you're family and all, I'm gonna make you a reasonable proposition . . . alright?"

She nodded and he went on: "Now just you understand this first, girl—I ain't gonna force you or anything . . . but, I'm only gonna keep you alive for as long as you make yourself useful around here. And right at this moment, what I need most of all is sexual gratification. You think you can maybe help me out with that? You're a smart girl, Sylvia Stewart, so just ask yourself this simple question: am I gonna suck my Uncle Ronan's penis like a lollypop or am I gonna die like an idiot, like that other yelling bitch did? Otherwise"—he jerked his thumb across at the plants—"those things are gonna have you for their lunch." He grabbed her chin and jerked her face up. "Do you get me?"

"YES!" she gasped in agony. Him pulling her head upward was moving her hands too, yanking them along the nails so the blood began flowing from their punctures again. "YES, YES!"

Ronan smiled. "Smart girl. So now, we're gonna be lovers, not relatives. You suck dick or die." He frowned. "Just don't let Cathy know what I'm doing to you—she's naïve and innocent and I doubt she'd approve." He jerked on Sylvia's chin until she gasped her agreement.

Then, while tears streamed from her eyes, Ronan stuck his foot-long piebald penis into Sylvia's mouth. The three pallets he'd placed her on had her mouth at just the right height for fellatio. Gripping her ears with both hands, he began thrusting back and forth. With his dappled manhood now as thick as a child's arm, Sylvia's mouth was a tight, almost unpleasant fit. Also, her teeth kept scraping on him. But after a while Ronan got into the feel of things. He grinned at Sylvia's tears. Her agony just got him harder.

Finally, Ronan thrust deep into the back of Sylvia's throat till she was choking, ejaculated so much semen that her neck bulged out as she swallowed it down, then, after giving her a brief respite to catch her breath so she didn't die on him (and during which streams of lumpy blue come regurgitated out between her gasping lips), he stuck the already re-stiffened penis back into her mouth and they went again. At least he did.

"Maybe I'll pull the nails out so I can plug your ass too," he mused as he thrust the fat pink-and-blue organ in and out between her lips and bulging cheeks. Blood was now dribbling from all six of the holes he'd made through her extremities.

For the moment though he concentrated on her mouth, each time jamming his penis in so deep that her eyes bulged, then pulling it out again just before she passed out from oxygen deprivation.

For her part, Sylvia, her chin and breasts smeared with blue semen, just kept crying and crying and crying.

Her agony worked on Ronan like Viagra.

CHAPTER 38

Ben

When Ben woke up that Sunday morning, at first he didn't move at all. He lay in bed thinking. The 'weakening drug' had worn off in the night. He both felt better and yet still unlike his usual self.

Cathy had spent most of the night with him. The girl had been sexually ravenous. She'd repeatedly demanded cunnilingus from him, and later when he felt stronger, full intercourse. Ben had obliged her, catching a few minutes of sleep between each sexual episode till she roused him again. He could still taste the strange sweetness of her vagina on his lips.

But she'd worried him a lot too. Not just her insatiability. Each time they'd made love, he'd gotten the feeling that she was being driven by an evil force; possessed as it were.

Cathy had finally slipped away at 5 a.m., telling him she didn't want her father to miss her in the farmhouse.

Ben had been glad to see her go. If he'd been weak when she'd found him, the endless sex had drained him even further.

***

Ben had slept. Once again he'd dreamt of the TALL man who looked like a Mexican Johnny Cash. The man had been pointing at Ben and laughing uproariously at something . . .

***

Now, upstairs in the middle barn, Ben lay in bed thinking. Warm sunlight streamed in through the window. He was lying on his back with his eyes shut.

He began smiling to himself.

Ben Hiller had just realized that he was rich. At least potentially rich.

At the moment no one else knew that Snort and Liza were dead.

May their souls find no rest in Hell, Ben thought grimly.

And, knowing he was about to commit murder, Snort had been careful to park his car well off the road. The State Police couldn't have found the car yet.

Ben knew where Snort kept his drug money. He didn't/couldn't take it to the bank. The cash was in a secret compartment in his bedroom, behind the wardrobe where the plasterboard had been ripped out. Snort had two hundred grand stashed in there, wrapped in tin foil so the rats didn't start eating it.

$200,000. Ready for whomever got to it first.

Ben intended to be that first person.

All I gotta do is survive this farm. Once I'm certain last night's craziness is over, I'm out of here and RICH. I'll just take over Snort's pot supply connections and clients. I'll run the east side of Springfield. I'll be swimming in the green! All I gotta do right now is survive; make it alive off of this crazy farm with its red-eyed decapitating monsters!

Grinning, Ben now opened his eyes and sat up. He did both in a single motion, so he didn't notice anything wrong till he was already upright.

Then he howled out loud: "What the damn hell!?"

The shirt and pants that Cathy had brought him were draped over the chair in the corner. Ben had seen no point in putting the clothes on when he'd have to repeatedly take them off again to have sex with her. As a result, he was completely naked and could see his body clearly.

"What the—?"

His entire body was swollen to twice its normal size and was a pale bluish-gray color. Every part of him was as lumpy as if he'd had fat injections. In line with the rest of this crazy transformation, his penis was at least twice as long as before, seemed thicker too, and both it and the skin of his thighs was mottled with dark blue skin.

When Ben squeezed what looked like a boil on his thigh, it exploded and wept a disgusting yellow pus like runny egg yolk down his leg. The sore didn't hurt.

He sat there horrified and confused, trying to work out how this had happened.

Ben finally realized that Cathy's vagina had poisoned him. He winced. *I knew her hole didn't smell and taste right. A pussy should smell fishy and taste slightly sour, not taste sweet like someone spilled sugar in it. And the secretion should be a milky white, not transparent blue. There's something alien about Cathy down there, and now it's infected me.*

He stood up. It took a lot of effort. His swollen body didn't feel like it belonged to him anymore. Even more worrying, it seemed to have swollen a little more since he'd first noticed the problem.

What the hell do I do now? I gotta get out of here and find a doctor fast. 'Cos if I don't, I can just kiss all of Snort's hidden money goodbye! No, I just need to get to hospital. Once the doctors see this, they'll know—shit!

While thinking, he'd shambled over to the window and looked down. This upstairs window faced out over a massive field of sunflowers. There was a large pond too, sandwiched between borders of sunflowers and looking like a giant mirror placed flat on them. Farther into the distance, Ben saw what looked like an old barn.

But it was what he'd noticed closer to him that made him now duck back out of sight.

He'd seen two of the red-eyes. The black creatures were walking away from the barn. One of them was carrying a severed human arm, the other a severed human head.

Ben sat on the bed shivering. Escaping this insane place might be more difficult than he'd thought. *I've no frigging idea what's going on here and I don't wanna know. I just wanna leave here alive and get to the money!*

It was at that moment that Cathy came in. She'd brought him some breakfast.

Her eyes immediately took in the changes in his appearance. "What happened to you, baby?" she asked. "You look different, like you got fat overnight."

"I've no idea. I feel different too."

She crossed over to the table and put the tray of food down. Then she turned to look at him. She walked across to the bed, discarding her dress as she did so. "It's alright, I like you this way too. Let's do it quick, then I gotta go help my dad. Then, when he's left I can sneak you off the farm."

Ben was about telling her to go to hell. But three things stopped him. The first thing was his realization that he needed her help. The second was his realization that she too looked different this morning. She was paler—with a bluish tint to her skin—and also had two weird pinkish lumps on her forehead. And though she was still slim and very shapely, with great breasts, her crotch and thighs were as piebald with dark blue as his were. (This clearly confirmed that she'd given him his current infection.)

The third thing was Ben's realization that seeing Cathy naked had given him a massive erection.

"See?" the blond girl said happily, pushing him back onto the bed. "You're delighted to see me."

There was no question about that. Ben's penis was something a horse would have been proud of, and ridiculously thick too. And it seemed as hard as the stone the red-eyes were made of.

The penis's size didn't deter Cathy one bit. She scampered up on top of Ben and let herself down onto the huge organ, gasping in delight as it sank into her sex. Ben was surprised when it all vanished inside her. He was even more surprised that she seemed to have additional space inside her little body to accommodate more of him if necessary.

She began bouncing up and down on him, looking like a piece of machinery rising and falling on a piston. Her nipples were a vivid blue against the paler curves of her young breasts. Ben tried to hold her breasts. This was too much effort, so he grabbed her buttocks instead.

"Yeah, baby," she moaned as she rode him. "This won't take too long, man. I just need to get this teenage angst out of my system. You've no idea what it's like being a teenager on the verge of twenty and living on a secluded farm with your dad."

After a while she came loudly. Breathless with ecstasy, she continued riding Ben till he came too. When she got off his penis, a torrent of blue ejaculate poured out of her.

Ben didn't know which bothered him more: the fact that his manhood had stayed hard after he'd come so much, or the fact that Cathy wasn't bothered in the least by the blue color of his semen.

Instead, Cathy smiled and kissed him sweetly on the lips. She tried gripping his penis with one hand, but her fingers could only encircle it halfway, so she used both hands, stroking up and down along the engorged shaft, which seemed at least four inches thick now.

"I'd love some more of this right away," she giggled, removing her hands from his penis and licking the blue semen from them, "but I've a lot of chores to attend to, and—hey, hey, baby, what's the matter with you?"

Ben had begun jerking and twitching and flailing about on the bed. He didn't need Cathy to tell him that he'd begun swelling up again. He could feel himself getting bigger by the second, inflating as if being pumped full of air. The swelling up hurt badly. And the fatter he got, the more piebald his body became, the more boils that covered it and burst open and spilled their yolky contents.

"Shit!" Cathy gasped in horror. "Oh my gosh. I wasn't expecting this to happen to you, man. I'm sorry—I really, really am."

All Ben could say was, "Help me!" and even this came out all garbled. He was horrified and confused. Even more puzzling, he didn't understand how come Cathy now had two horns sticking out of her forehead. Red horns. Right where those weird pink lumps had been.

"Help . . . help me!" he cried, as his body and manhood puffed up yet again to horrendous proportions.

"I don't know what to do!" Cathy yelped in fright. Then she turned and ran out of the room, scooping up her dress and flip-flops on the way, but forgetting to lock him in.

Ben heard the sound of her panicked footsteps descending the barn stairs. He lay there in pain, swelling larger by the minute, thinking of the lovely drug money waiting for him if he could just escape from this crazy farm.

She grew horns! Horns!

CHAPTER 39

Michael & Darrin

"Where the hell can she be?" Michael asked Darrin.

They'd been searching the forest for Sharon for an hour now.

Though perfectly normal on the surface, the forest struck them both as being 'wrong' in some way.

This 'wrong' was nothing they could put a finger on. They saw nothing out of the ordinary. Just trees and grass and flowers and the occasional bird and butterfly and grasshopper. A plague of red and gray squirrels. A pair of raccoons had bolted on seeing them. Likewise three white-tailed deer.

But it was there all right, mingled in with the pleasant summer green and the color riot of fifty brilliant summer blossoms, an upsetting feeling that seemed to float on the cooling breezes; an inexplicable but nonetheless terrifying sensation, like the sudden touch of someone else's fingers on one's neck in a pitch-black room, when you knew you'd locked the door and were all alone in there.

Neither man said a word about what he felt. They had no need to speak, no need to convey their rising dread by either word or gesture. In this particular instance, their unvoiced communication had elements of telepathy in it.

"Maybe Sharon's hiding from us," Darrin suggested.

"Hiding?"

Darrin leaned against a tree and wiped his forehead with a hand. The weather had turned hot now and they'd both begun sweating. "You know, maybe she thinks we've found out about herself and Vanni and—"

"Why would she think that?"

Darrin shrugged. "I'm just suggesting. If she talks in her sleep, or maybe accidentally cried out my wife's name while you two were doing it? You didn't notice at all, but she realizes she did and thinks you did and . . ."

"Oh, no," Michael said, a worried look coming over his face. "I never thought of that. Sharon gets really emotional at times. Let's hope she didn't come out here just to hang herself from one of these trees."

He hurried off, yelling, "Sharon, baby! Honey, I'm not angry at you! I'm not angry at all!"

Perplexed himself and subdued by the forest's heavy ambience, Darrin hurried after him.

CHAPTER 40

Vanni

Vanni waited and waited and waited for someone to come back to the farmhouse.

No one did. It was crazy, as if everyone had vanished into thin air.

First Vanni got worried, then she got bored. Then she got angry. It would have been different had she been able to watch TV or log into social media on her phone. But the TV only showed plains of peppersalt static and her phone gave her continuous 'Mobile Network Unavailable' and 'Unable to connect to internet, please check your connections' messages.

She got up and paced awhile, from the living room to the front porch and back again. *Where has everyone gotten to? Cathy, for one, should have been back here an hour ago. And what's keeping Darrin and Michael?*

Finally she climbed the stairs. After looking out of she and Darrin's bedroom window and making sure she understood how to get to the pond and wouldn't get lost on the way, she slipped into a white bikini, slung a towel around her neck, then returned downstairs.

I'm going sunbathing, she thought angrily. *When everyone gets back from looking for Sharon, they can start looking for me instead. It isn't like we'll be leaving immediately they all return anyway. Ronan still has to wake up, then drive into town for the auto mechanic. Lots of time to work on my tan.*

She walked out of the rear farmhouse door and directly into the sunflower field.

She wasn't trying to conceal herself though. About a hundred and twenty feet in from the point where the nearer pond–field border met the main inner farm route was a short pier to which was tethered a red rowboat. Vanni had calculated that cutting through the sunflower field would shorten her walk by about fifty yards compared to if she took the path.

As she stepped into the field, Vanni noticed a darker patch of soil at its border. Reddish and still a little wet. *Hmm,* she thought, *this looks like blood. Most likely spilled hog's blood.* She tried to remember if Sylvia had mentioned her uncle rearing pigs on his farm.

She forgot the blood. In the distance, she could hear what sounded like baaing sheep; the noises coming maybe from the last barn. Splashes of blood on an animal farm meant nothing.

But now Vanni had a second question: If you had sheep, weren't you supposed to have sheepdogs too? So far, during her short time on the Higgins Farm, she not seen any dogs. So where were they? Locked in with the other animals or in the kennels behind the barns that Ronan had mentioned? But then she'd hear them barking for sure. Alright, now that she thought about it, Vanni *had* heard some dogs barking earlier; just that the animals had sounded quite far off.

She let that go too. Ronan's hounds were most likely asleep. Dogs liked sleeping.

She walked through the sunflowers and immediately encountered a third oddity: A large number of those plants closest to the farmyard were burnt. This struck Vanni as odd because the charred patches on the plants were spaced randomly on them. She couldn't think of any kind of fire that would scorch the plants in such a haphazard fashion.

The swath of six-foot-high stalks soon obstructed her from being seen from the farm track. Vanni, however, could still clearly make out the tops of the barns, which reassured her that she wouldn't get lost.

Now she was deep inside the field, the sunflowers' non-floral scent surrounding her. She had the clear impression that she should be terrified of something. But she didn't know what she should be frightened of.

It was in this frame of mind that she stepped out of the sunflower field onto the pond shore.

She looked around. The wooden pier extended thirty feet out into the water. The red rowboat was secured to its right side, with a pair of oars inside the vessel. On Vanni's left, a thin grass border extended from the pier to the farm path, a four-foot-broad walkway along the water's edge.

The pond itself stretched a hundred yards across to its opposite shore, where the sunflower field resumed. Above that endless carpet of flowers—green stalks and leaves, yellowish-orange blossoms—rose the distant barn where Cathy had supposedly gone to search for Sharon.

On Vanni's left, the pond extended forty yards to the road. Across the road the right side of the third barn was visible. To the right of the barn lay a wide expanse of thick woodland. On Vanni's right, the pond extended for a hundred yards before curving west and out of sight, forming the 'L' shape one noticed from the farmhouse windows.

Vanni walked ten feet onto the wooden pier and spread her towel. Then she lay on her back to catch the sun, her hands folded under her head.

She still felt worried, and as far as she could tell, for no reason at all.

For a moment she felt pure terror, a descending blackness as if her mind was fragmenting and her sanity was slipping away. And then, as suddenly as it had arrived, the psyche-shredding panic was gone, no longer even a figment of her imagining.

What is wrong with me? I'm the only one out here!

She shut her eyes, forced herself to relax. The terror resisted, but she persisted. After a while she succeeded. Her thoughts floated to her romance with Sharon.

Of course, Sharon hadn't been Vanni's first female lover. Far from it. Vanni had hooked up with girls before. But those were all long in the past, long before she'd met Darrin. Since then, she'd been totally faithful and committed to Darrin. She'd not once felt the urge for another woman's body. To her practical mind, getting laid was getting laid; so long as she had penis she didn't need vagina.

Vanni just liked *sex*—man or woman, it didn't matter who with.

Her affair with Sharon was still deeply enjoyable but must end soon. Or else their husbands would find out. And she'd be divorced and starting from romantic scratch. It wasn't worth it.

So, it's time to return to Dick City fulltime. But, ooh, baby, visiting Pussy Paradise was great fun while it lasted.

The bittersweet knowledge of she and Sharon's inevitable parting had gotten her sexually aroused. After a quick peek to determine that no one watching from the farm route could possibly realize what she was doing, Vanni slipped her fingers into her bikini bottom and began masturbating.

Pleasant images of Sharon's breasts filled her mind. Keeping her eyes closed, she relaxed into the pleasure and enjoyed herself. She quickly conjured up an intense erotic fantasy of Sharon giving her cunnilingus.

This was why Vanni didn't at first realize she wasn't alone anymore.

***

Fingers deep inside herself, she smelt it. Something burning close by.

Her mind immediately went to the strange patterns scorched onto the sunflowers at the point where she'd entered the field.

Sensing danger, she opened her eyes and sat up. She'd lain down with her feet facing the start of the pier and as such immediately saw her peril.

What the hell are . . . ?

Four humanoid creatures, each blacker than night and with no facial features other than massive red eyes that shone like vehicle brake lights, stood at the foot of the pier. Their glowing red eyes were staring right at her.

Yelping in fright, Vanni leapt to her feet. Once again she felt that insane terror she'd recently experienced, only now she knew what she was terrified of.

How the hell didn't I hear them coming!? Oh, because I was about coming too!

The burning heat she'd smelt was coming from the black creatures. The first step one of them took onto the pier confirmed this. The pier wood around its foot instantly blackened and began smoking. The black foot had only two malformed toes.

"Stay away from me!" Vanni yelped.

Instead, another one of them stepped forward onto the pier. Then a third. Now the wood actually did catch fire around their feet. She also realized now that each of the black creatures had a fire burning inside its body too, the flames clearly visible through cracks in each ebony torso.

One thing was certain: Vanni wasn't waiting for them to reach her.

She saw only one chance of escaping the monsters and took it.

She leapt into the pond. The water wasn't deep where she landed, just about three feet high, reaching just above her hips. She was glad she'd not dived in head-first and tried to swim away. In the current circumstances that might have been disastrous.

Barefoot now, she waded quickly through the water, away from the pier. The black creatures didn't strike her as being able to move particularly fast. She figured she'd reach the road and escape to the farmhouse before they caught her.

Then, hearing a loud splash, Vanni looked back and almost pissed herself in fright.

All three of the creatures on the pier had leapt into the water after her. The pond boiling and steaming around their black bodies, they waded towards her.

Vanni didn't expect what happened next.

Just like that, all three of the creatures exploded. They blew up like massive fireworks, their arms and legs and heads and torsos flying in different directions. Three balls of fire rose simultaneously skyward, splashed down again a distance away, and re-exploded.

The boom of the monsters' destruction echoed over the pond surface, rolling like thunder fallen to earth. Before this first wave of noises ceased, lesser continuations arose from those points where the creatures' body parts had splashed into the water.

Vanni had ducked as a sizzling black head flew over her. Now she stood gaping, mouth open in disbelief. *What just happened?*

She didn't gape long though. Whatever the reason for her reprieve, she intended to make the most of it. Besides, she could see the fourth red-eyed monster, the one that hadn't leapt into the water, already waking down the grassy pond verge towards her.

Well, it can't get into the water! Ha ha!

She stepped up to where the water was only about a foot deep, then ran through it toward the farm road and the barns.

She'd have screamed for help, only she remembered everyone had seemingly vanished and no one would hear her.

Almost as if her previous premonition was preparation for this, she felt her sanity threatening to depart her again. She gripped her head tight, as if trying to keep her mind safely locked inside it.

CHAPTER 41

Ben

She grew horns! Cathy grew horns!

Ben got to his feet. Swollen everywhere as he was now, this wasn't easy. Each step, each motion, hurt like he was dying. But still, he couldn't die in here like this. Better he dare the red-eyes.

For the moment at least, he'd stopped growing larger. Ben was bulky and bulbous and blue all over, but his crazy transformation seemed to have halted. Or at least to have hit some biological roadblock and paused.

Which gave him some hope.

She left the door unlocked. All I need is a doctor. A good caring doctor.

He made his agonized way to the door and let himself out of it. Then began the immensely painful process of descending the stairs. Step by slow painful step.

As Ben moved, bits of reeking blue flesh dropped off his mountainous bulk.

The resulting wounds burnt like hellfire.

CHAPTER 42

Vanni

With the red-eyed monster in pursuit, Vanni burst out onto the road.

The farmhouse lay a hundred yards to her left. She doubted she'd be able to reach it before the monster exited the pondside trail. She didn't want it knowing which way she'd gone.

Directly in front of her stood the third barn. She ran towards it instead.

She reached it, found it locked, and without trying to see if she could get the door open, turned and ran left towards the middle barn, the door of which was wide open.

She ducked through the barn entrance. The barn lights were off and it was dim inside; a vale of shadows. Great. Perfect to hide in. Vanni tugged the door shut behind her. Then she opened it up a crack and peeped out.

She'd hidden just in time. The red-eyed monster was just emerging from the pond trail.

She watched it. It stood there by the pond shore with its head swiveling left and right, a black stone robot waiting for orders.

Now Vanni had time to feel terrified. As the fear rose in her, she quickly looked around her surroundings for a weapon. She couldn't make out much amidst all the shadows, but still, almost immediately she spotted a machete lying on a wooden crate nearby. She ran over and picked the machete up. It was dusty but sharp.

Now armed, she returned to stare out through the barn door again.

She saw no sign of her horrible pursuer. For the moment at least, the burning black monster had vanished.

Vanni relaxed. *Okay, I'll wait here till I either see Cathy coming back this way or my husband comes looking for me.*

At the edges of her consciousness, she felt terror threatening to consume her again. Vanni was as brave as the next person in line, but this? What did human notions of courage count for when one faced something outside of human experience?

She hefted her machete and studied its blade. *I don't even know what those black things were. Or why they exploded on entering the pond. I just know I'm safe now and that's how I plan on remaining.*

"Her . . . her mer!" a voice groaned behind her.

Startled and scared, Vanni spun around at the noise. Then she shrieked in utter terror again.

It was at this exact point that Vanni began losing her mind.

There was a monster approaching her. It was blue, taller than she was, and obscenely fat, with piebald blue skin as patchy as a giraffe's. A wet Mohawk of blonde hair topped its head. Its face was a small area of crumpled features in the center of its two-foot-wide head. Swellings covered its body; from them dripped a disgusting egg-yolk liquid.

Vanni had never seen anything as repulsive as this in her life.

"Help!" the creature groaned. "I'm in agony!" As it spoke, chunks of dripping blue flesh fell off its belly and splattered on the ground.

Its voice wasn't even recognizable as human. Nor was what it said. "Her! I me anni!" was what Vanni heard, the phrase tumbling like vomit from an overstretched mouth dotted with widely-spaced teeth.

The monster seemed to have three legs. Then Vanni realized that the third leg was actually the creature's penis dragging on the floor. The mottled, vein-riddled organ was eight inches thick. A lumpy blue slime from the penis's tip trailed behind it.

What on earth!?

"H'l m'lis!" it pleaded again. "I ne a 'ctor!"

If Vanni heard pain and anguish in the creature's slurpy noises, they didn't stir up pity in her. She was too frightened. All she saw was yet another hideous monster reaching out to grab her. To hurt and kill her.

Only now, she was armed. And dangerous. Worst of all, the portion of her mind that had been keeping her sane was overloading.

The blue monster stepped toward her. It reached for her with enormous hands that seemed waterlogged. As she stared, a long split appeared in the creature's left forearm. Then all the skin and flesh below the split fell open like a flap and swung freely. She could see the forearm bones, yellow and wet with something that wasn't blood.

"H'l m'lis!"

Vanni screamed, feeling madness coming over her. With the machete raised overhead, she ran at the thing. She slammed the machete down hard into the monster's head. Then again, from a different angle this second time, as though she were cutting a giant cake or jumbo pizza.

When she jerked the machete back again, a quarter of the thing's head fell out of its skull. That quarter contained one of its tiny eyes. She saw pink brains in its head. Bluish blood gushed from the wound.

The monster screamed.

She screamed too, terrified of the efficacy of her own violence.

The creature meanwhile wobbled on its revolting piebald legs. Though she'd killed it, it didn't fall over. It couldn't fall over: the unbelievable length and girth of its penis—reaching to the ground the way it did—meant that it was balanced on a tripod.

Seeing it upright like that, Vanni believed it was still alive. She was scared it might heal itself and attack her again, so she instead attacked it first. A preemptive strike. She began swinging wildly at it, chopping madly at whichever part of it caught her eye and fancy.

It fell apart in bits. Arms, legs, more chunks of head—whatever she hit dropped to the ground.

However, as it fragmented beneath her relentless assault, so too did her mind. Vanni was vaguely aware that she was losing psychic parts of herself, but she was powerless to stop her sanity from decomposing and draining away. This was too far outside of anything anyone could expect; her brain had no defenses against it.

On this physical plane she fought heroically, but her psyche had long ago been defeated, its disintegration starting the moment she'd first sighted the red-eyes walking onto the pier.

Vanni swung passionately, stepping in close to her quarry. Its gore drenched her as she butchered it. Her white bikini quickly stained blue with the monster's blood. Shreds of its blue flesh plastered her all over.

She only stopped hacking at it when its entire top half lay in chunks at her feet. Its bottom half was still upright though. Vanni placed her bare foot against the root of its penis and kicked hard, taking satisfaction when the 'three legs' also toppled over into the piled mess that she'd made of the rest of it.

She stood amidst the creature's wreckage, breasts heaving from the effort, her arms aching; a warrior goddess dyed blue from blonde hair to muddy toes.

But she was a goddess lacking an ice pack to cool her fevered brain.

CHAPTER 43

Michael & Darrin

"Dude, I really think we should turn back. There's no way Sharon could've walked this far. What on earth could she possibly want out here?"

"Yeah, I ain't even sure we're still on the farm anymore. She's likely back at the farmhouse already and everyone's begun worrying about us instead."

"It's these damn phones. If they worked we could at least call ahead and learn what the situation is now."

The two concerned husbands turned around and retraced their steps. However, surrounded by trees that were more or less identical in shape and size, they ended up losing their way and returning by a route slightly different from that by which they'd entered the forest.

They stumbled on, startling small forest animals, pushing branches and leaves out of their way.

They were about to have a fateful encounter.

CHAPTER 44

Vanni

Her machete dripping with blue gore, Vanni stepped backward out of the monster's remains. A part of her mind wanted to go on chopping it up, but she restrained herself. With what sanity she had left, she cautioned herself. There might be more monsters out there, and they might need killing too. She needed to conserve her strength.

So she turned and walked over to open the barn door and leave. She wasn't hiding anymore. She'd walk in plain sight to the farmhouse. And God Almighty help whoever or whatever was so stupid as to attack her.

But the barn door was flung open before she reached it.

Cathy walked in.

"Ha, I got you now, bitch," she growled on seeing Vanni. "I saw you run in here and . . ." She gasped on seeing the blue monster's dead remains and Vanni's dripping blade. "What have you done to Ben? Shit—you killed Ben!?"

Vanni made no reply. Her thoughts ground like unoiled gears in her head. *Ben? Who the hell is Ben? This thing I killed wasn't human.*

Vanni looked at Cathy herself and more of her mental integrity unraveled. Cathy was yet more oddity to deal with. Somewhere deep in Vanni's head the tiny nub that remained of her 'sanity switch' was being eroded away by this ceaseless flood of wonders.

See, Cathy looked different now. Though still a blonde, her skin was bright blue and she had two long red horns growing from her temples. Her arms looked like someone had painted them over in overlapping shades of light and dark blue; and her nose looked plump and rather pointy.

One more monster to deal with, Vanni thought dully.

"I'm gonna kill you, bitch!" Cathy screamed and charged at her.

Vanni calmly waited for the girl to come. Then, with a loud yell of her own, she slammed her machete sideways, hard into Cathy's neck, slicing her head clean off.

Cathy's head sailed through the air, hit the nearby barn wall and bounced back to rest beside the open door. It landed on its side with its eyes open.

Her body collapsed.

Vanni smiled. Yes, that was five monsters she'd dispatched today. *I'm getting pretty good at this.*

At this point, it might still have been possible for Vanni to reclaim her frayed mind. With the help of a sympathetic psychiatrist and months of therapy, she might have returned to normal, become sane again.

But then Cathy's head opened its eyes. And her body sat up and began feeling around itself as if looking for its head.

Cathy's head stared at Vanni with eyes full of hatred.

"You stupid slut bitch," Cathy growled. "Once I'm back together again, I'm going to kill you for real." She laughed nastily. "And then I'm gonna feed you to dad's creepy plants myself."

The severed head ceased laughing. Instead, a look of intense concentration now came over its blue features. The headless body got up off the floor and shambled towards it.

That was it for Vanni. It wasn't fear that had done her in, simply her stacked incomprehension of all that she'd just experienced.

Her mind breaking for good, she ran out of the barn with the machete still in her hand. She ran right across the path and into the sunflower field, gibbering insanely and chopping down any sunflower plants that blocked her way.

CHAPTER 45

Cathy

After the crazed Vanni had run off, Cathy Higgins put herself together again.

She mentally willed her body to pick up her head and place it back on her neck. After she'd correctly positioned her head, she sat on a dusty crate to allow her wound heal.

Cathy didn't feel at all odd about her strange new capabilities. She just took them for granted. 'Uncle Bargainer' had explained to she and her father that they'd both be very hard—if not impossible—to kill from now on. An unforeseen but not unwelcome side-effect due to a reaction between the elixir that had revived her and the secretions of the hell-plants her father was growing.

The blue skin and red horns *did* bother her. Those were surely going to attract attention. She'd have to ask Uncle Bargainer to revert her looks back to normal.

While her neck repaired itself, Cathy stared moodily at Ben's remains. All that blue and purple and yellow mess. She'd really liked Ben.

Finally she shrugged. *He's long dead and gone, way beyond fixing. I doubt if even Uncle Bargainer could resurrect him. Oh, what a waste. Nothing to do now but feed him to dad's plants.*

That decided, Cathy got to her feet. Her neck wasn't completely joined yet, but it was repaired enough that her head wouldn't fall back off.

She strode out of the barn, grumbling, "Now where the hell did that damn red-eye walk off to? I need it to come clean up Ben's remains."

CHAPTER 46

Michael, Darrin & . . .

"Once we're back in Boston," Darrin said as they pushed through the forest, "we ain't going directly home. Hell no, man. I'm driving us four over to a seafood restaurant where we're gonna forget all about this damn Higgins Farm."

Michael grunted assent. He felt moody, worried. He hoped Sharon would be waiting when they got back to the farmhouse. Because if she wasn't . . .

"Yeah," Darrin went on enthusiastically, "we're gonna have us oysters and lobsters and . . . and ice cold beer! Beer so chilled, the condensation runs down the damn bottle like a waterfall of raindrops. Because . . ."

And then Darrin yelped "Yeow!" and vanished.

Michael snapped out of his gloom and spun around. "What?"

"Shit! Shit!" Darrin was yelping from somewhere out of sight. "Who left this damn hole here? Hey, Mike, I'm underground!"

Michael found Darrin a moment later. His friend had fallen into a pit in the forest floor. The hole was about six feet deep and four feet wide.

Only thing was, Darrin wasn't the only one in the hole. There was a young woman in there too. It was sheer luck that Darrin hadn't severely wounded the girl when he'd dropped in on her. As it was, his elbow had stunned her. Hitting her though had broken his fall and kept him from breaking his ankles.

Nothing more was said until Michael had pulled them both out of the hole.

Then he and Darrin realized that they knew the girl. "Amy F-F-Fox?" Darrin sputtered. "D-DJ Amy Fox?"

The platinum blonde head nodded dully. She was still stunned. "Yeah. The badass queen of the turntables. Still alive after enduring three lifetime's worth of crap in one night."

"I'm Darrin and he's Michael."

"Thanks for dropping by," Amy said. "I've been needing company for ages."

"But, but, what happened?" Michael asked her, pointing to the hole in the forest floor. "How'd you get down there? We heard you guys all packed up and left after the fight last night."

"Yeah," Darrin added. "So, how come you're still here?"

No one needed to tell either man that something had gone badly wrong with Amy Fox. She was completely disheveled. She had dirt and twigs and grass and leaves in her silver hair, her makeup was smeared all over her face, and her white pantsuit was ripped up. She was also barefoot and her feet were bloody and seemed cut up from running.

Amy Fox sighed at their questions. "You're never gonna believe what happened."

"We're looking for Mike's missing wife," Darrin explained. "We've been looking through this forest for two hours now and found no sign of her. I think if you know something that might help us find her— anything, no matter how bad—that you should tell us."

Amy laughed mirthlessly. "Okay then. How about monsters?"

"Monsters?"

She nodded. "His wife has likely gone where everyone else went. And I don't think any of them are gonna be coming back this way."

She felt somewhat disappointed that they didn't seem more surprised. But then, the forest's peculiarly unnatural ambience hung over the three of them now. Such an atmosphere forced belief on you.

Michael's face *had* however pinched up with worry. "Monsters? Amy, what are you talking about?"

Her own face seemed to crumple in on itself with memory. "See, last night monsters crashed Sylvia's birthday party and killed everyone. I've been hiding since then. I don't think anyone else survived the massacre."

"What!?"

"Just listen," Amy said. And then, still a little dazed, she patiently recounted to the two men everything that had happened the previous night, at least as much of it as she'd personally witnessed.

"And then I just ran, see?" she finished. "Two of them were after me, but I climbed a tree and they ran past. I think they killed two people—a man and a woman—seemed to be the pair who dug this hole. They grip people by their heads and the heads explode—just like that. I saw them dragging the headless bodies past." She paused to catch her breath. "I waited till all the screaming stopped. Then I climbed down out of the tree, and went to see if anyone had survived the slaughter. I hadn't even left the woods yet when more of the things came after me, this time led by the farmer's daughter Cathy, who was painted up like a psycho clown and was clutching two bloody knives. I turned and ran again. I wasn't watching where I was heading— actually it was too dark to see where I was going anyway. That's how I fell into this hole." She tenderly felt a bump on the back of her head. "The fall knocked me out. Thank God it didn't break my neck."

"Shit!" Michael said, his face white. "Are you serious that this actually happened?"

She looked at him without rancor. "C'mon, man, gimme a break, wilya? I'm a celebrity. Do you think I make a habit of looking like shit and falling into holes in the woods?"

"It was a party," Darrin said seriously. "Amy, you're a self-confessed party animal. You could have gotten wasted on hallucinogens."

She looked like she'd get angry. But then she smiled coldly. "You're right, I could have been stoned. But, hell no, dude, I wasn't. You can be sure of that 'cos what saved my life was that I'd ducked down from the stage—I'd put on a long mixtape that would give me half-an-hour off: I do that when I need to take a pee or shit—and went to my DJ tent to snort some coke and pop an E. That's what I was about doing when the screaming started. I peeped out and saw people having their heads blown up and their guts torn out by those black things. And if you want proof that I'm telling you the truth . . ." She felt around in her ripped pants and pulled out two plastic baggies. One was half-filled with white powder, the second had five blue tablets in it with 'Skype' stamped on them. "I hadn't even opened either of them. I just stuffed them in my pocket and ran barefoot through the sunflowers. It wasn't until I burst out near the barns that the red-eyed things saw me and came after me too."

"Shit," Darrin said.

"Shit," Michael agreed.

"More like a rain of sheep shit," Amy Fox corrected them. "You really need to have been there and seen it. I'd never have believed something like that could ever happen at a party I was working in a million billion trillion zillion quadrillion years."

CHAPTER 47

Amy Fox, with Michael & Darrin

Amy Fox wasn't a person to take shit from anyone or anything. She was a fighter; that was simply her basic makeup. It was how she'd become so successful in the music industry. But since yesterday night, fighting had seemed out of the question. Flight had been the sensible action to take.

The problem in this situation was that even escaping seemed impossible. Since yesterday, Amy had had no idea which direction to walk in to avoid the danger.

"Come with me," she told her two male companions. "I wanna show you guys something."

They followed her through the woods. Both men were perplexed. Michael was trying to think up a plan of action, but hadn't yet come up with anything.

Monsters? One thing was certain: neither man disbelieved Amy's story. Suspension of disbelief had been building in them both all morning, they just hadn't been aware of it.

Amy led them to a break in the trees. They came out directly opposite the pond, with sunflower fields on both sides of it. On their own right were the three barns leading back to the farmhouse.

"I had no idea we were so close to where we started," Michael said.

"Shush and watch," Amy cautioned. She pointed left. "Just watch that huge barn over there. And keep quiet. If they notice you, you're on your own."

Amy, Darrin and Michael sat just inside the tree line and watched.

"What are we watching for?" Darrin asked after a while.

"Patience. You'll know when you see it."

Almost like she'd called it forth from the building, a ten or twelve foot high black figure stepped out of the distant barn.

"Hey," Darrin said with a little shiver. "That's the guy we met on our way to the turnoff. The Mexican-looking one."

Amy looked surprised. "You know him?" The tall figure was now walking away from the farmhouse; towards the woods, but not in their direction.

"Yeah, we've met," Michael replied. "He's the one who told us he saw my wife heading into the woods. Then he vanished like he was never there to start with. Who is he anyway?"

She scowled like she was angry and plucked twigs and debris from her platinum hair. "I don't know and I don't wanna know. What I do know is that he keeps coming and going from that barn over there. He's there like once each hour. And . . . that barn is where all the corpses were carried off to last night. While hiding in my tree I saw them being taken over there."

The gaunt giant figure had now vanished from sight.

"Amy, how can you know that?" Michael asked now the distant man had disappeared. "I mean, about the guy visiting there once an hour? You've been inside that hole since last night, haven't you?"

She shook her head. "I managed to climb out earlier, but then I saw some shit . . ."

"What did you see?"

"Okay, I was right here watching. I was thinking, if maybe I could make it across the sunflower field to my DJ tent and retrieve my phone and call for help. But just as I was about crossing the road I saw four of the red-hot black creatures—that brat Cathy calls them 'red-eyes'— well, they came down the lakeside in a rush. They don't seem to walk fast, but they can really move when they want to." She pointed at the pond. "So, then they turn inwards at the lake shore over there, and walk in between the lake and the fields. At first I was unsure where they were headed, then I noticed the pier and . . . I saw that there was a woman sunbathing on it."

"A woman?" Describe her."

"Tall, slim blonde, white swimsuit."

"Vanni." Darrin squeezed his lips tight. "That's my wife," he explained to Amy. "We asked her to wait for us in the farmhouse."

"What happened to her?" Michael asked.

"Nothing. She got away," Amy replied.

"She got away?" Darrin wheezed relief.

Amy nodded. "I'm still surprised by what happened. The red-eyes almost got her—if you look you can still see part of the pier smoking from catching fire when they stepped up on it—but she jumped into the water to escape them. They jumped in too, and next thing, they all blew up." She made a 'expanding' gesture with her fingers. "Poof! Kaboom!—Like bombs."

"Blew up?"

"Yeah, like they were allergic to water or something."

"What happened to Vanni then?"

"Oh, she ran in the water to the road, then down to the farmhouse, I think."

"You didn't see for sure?"

Amy shook her head emphatically. "I didn't wait. I forgot to mention, man—only three of the frigging red-eyes got blown up by the water. The fourth one walked back out and stood in the road looking around. When it started towards me, I ran back to my hole and leapt inside it again. You guys showed up shortly afterwards."

"Well, that's one wife safe at least," Michael said. "Now we just need to find the other one."

"I'm still confused as hell about what to do," Darrin said.

"Only one thing we can do," Michael said. "And that's visit the old barn over there. From what Amy says, Sharon is likely being held captive in there."

"Shush!" Amy whispered. "Get under cover! One of them is coming now!"

They ducked back behind the trees.

A short while later, one of the red-eyes trudged into view, coming from the direction of the farmhouse.

Michael and Darrin confirmed that the creature was exactly as Amy had described it: black as night and with no facial features except for those two horrid burning eyes; and with long cracks in its torso and limbs that revealed the fires within.

The red-eye was pulling something after it, what looked like the remains of a huge blue reptile—just the lizard's legs and tail. The heat the red-eye gave off reached them under the trees.

They watched the black creature turn off the path into the sunflower field, making an unerring beeline for the distant barn. And was it just their fevered imaginations or did the sky over the barn look somehow different from that above the rest of the countryside, darker than it should be, tainted by whatever arcane uses the building was being put to?

"You guys convinced now?" Amy asked.

Darrin nodded. She looked at Michael.

He frowned at her. "I gotta visit that barn. I gotta rescue my wife."

"Sure, man," Amy agreed. "I'll come with you. I wanna see what's going on in there. It'll be hard to convince the cops to come do anything otherwise. One mention of monsters and they'll lock us up for wasting their time. But mention corpses and you've made their day."

They looked at Darrin. "You coming with us?"

He nodded. "Yeah. But we'll need to visit the farmhouse first so I can get my gun from my suitcase."

"Cool," Amy said, straightening her hair. "There may be other weapons in the farmhouse too. And, guys, watch out for Cathy. She's as crazy as Mardi Gras."

Darrin groaned. "Shit. Vanni's alone with her."

Michael got out his phone and began fiddling with it.

Amy scowled at him. "Hey, man, you know this place has no signal."

"True, but the phone camera still works. The cops want evidence, we'll give them some."

They left the forest and hurried towards the farmhouse.

CHAPTER 48

Michael, Darrin & Amy . . . Before the Storm

They found neither Vanni nor Cathy in the farmhouse.

"I can only assume Cathy caught Vanni and took her out to the barn before we got to the road earlier," Amy said.

Darrin scowled. "Let's get out there and find out for sure."

"Yeah," Michael agreed. "We're beginning to looking really careless here—the husbands who lost their wives."

Upstairs they found a Remington 870 pump-action shotgun and a box of shells.

Darrin loaded up the Remington and put the spare shells in his pocket. He handed his own Sig P220 to Michael, but Amy snatched it away from him.

"Trust me on this, baby: I can shoot way better than you," she told Michael with a cool wink.

Amy had changed her clothes, borrowing a set of Cathy's jeans and one of her tee shirts. "Her bras were all too small for me," she'd explained to the men when she imagined they were admiring her breasts. She'd nodded down at her nipples, which were pushing out the tee shirt as if she was sexually aroused. "I'm a big girl; can't help it if I bounce a lot."

Cathy's shoes were too small for her, but Vanni's sneakers fit her perfectly.

Now she tucked the pistol into her waistband. "I love big guns," she said. She had a gleam in her eyes, but it was born of anticipation, not chemical abuse. Amy felt excited that they were finally about doing something about this impossible situation, even if it that something was just to understand it before getting the hell out of here.

By force of habit, she moved her two baggies of drugs from her ripped white pantsuit to the pockets of the jeans she now had on. Shit was shit, but Amy wasn't prepared to let good drugs go to waste.

There was always tomorrow's party; so long as she survived today's nightmare.

Disarmed by Amy, Michael contented himself with a small axe he'd found in the broom closet.

They left for the barn.

Walking through the front yard, Amy was once more surprised that all the vehicles—her own Hyundai Tucson SUV included—had vanished. And, as a peek north from Cathy's bedroom window had revealed, so had the stage, the PA equipment, her CD and LP turntables and laptop and mixer, her record cases (which really angered her—she'd spent thousands of dollars amassing that record collection), her DJ tent, everything. The guys confirmed that everything had already been gone on their arrival here. But how? And to where? Who had stolen everything?

In addition to his axe, Michael was also carrying a plastic two-liter bottle of water.

"For what's hopefully the last of those red-eyes," he explained as they walked the dirt track between the barns and the sunflower field. "Amy, you said that last night there were thirty or forty of the creatures. But you've seen only four of them today, three of which got blown up in the pond. So I'm betting . . . no, I'm damn well praying that all the rest have left for home and that there's only one left now."

"Guns might work on them too," Darrin said hopefully.

"I'm not sure," Amy disagreed. "I think Mike's right. While hiding in my hole, I spent a lot of time pondering on why the ones that entered the water exploded like that. Crazy as it sounds to say, I think the red-eyes come from Hell, or from some hot infernal realm like it. They're fire creatures and really are allergic to water. At least to a lot of it."

She forced a grin. "Let's hope that that's enough water we're carrying, or we three may have to spit on the thing to make it blow up."

The joke relieved the tension a bit.

They caught hints of wood smoke on the wind, and faint animal smells also, both most likely coming from one of the barns beside them. Amy also smelt something 'doggy' in the air. She recalled Sylvia saying her uncle had shut up all his sheep in the third barn so the loud party music didn't agitate them.

They'd reached the pond. While they walked beside it, Michael called their attention to the red boat now floating free towards the pond's farther end. Neither of his companions was interested in either the placid gray body of water or the boat.

"Too bad this is just a pond and not a river leading off this damn place," Michael commented as they stepped past the water and back beside the sunflower field again, this time with the forest they'd previously hidden in forming the path's left border.

***

None of them, least of all her husband Darrin, suspected that Vanni was lying insane in that red boat so calmly floating away from them. Vanni was staring up at the blue sky, grinning and whispering gibberish sentences to the clouds and the sun. Occasionally she hung an arm over the side of the boat, dipping her fingers in the water and stirring it happily.

None of them suspected either that Michael's wife Sharon had been dead for three hours now and was, right at that very moment, being shoveled (in little 'bite-sized' chunks) as refill meat into one of Ronan's demon-plant's freshly-emptied tubs out in the barn that was their hellish destination.

***

"Yeah, here's where the red-eye went through," Amy said, pointing to the spot in the field where the sunflower stalks started looking burnt.

They stepped off the road and stealthily moved towards the barn.

CHAPTER 49

Cathy

Above all, none of three headed for the barn was aware that Cathy Higgins *had* been in the farmhouse when they'd arrived there.

She'd heard them come in, decided the three of them were too many to take on unassisted, and as such had quickly slipped out the back door and waited for them to leave the house.

At the moment Cathy was following the three of them at a safe distance, calculating the right moment to strike.

I really wish the phones worked right now, she thought in some anger. *Then I could call ahead and warn dad of the danger.*

CHAPTER 50

Amy

Now the world seemed scary to Amy. It seemed creepy. Everything about the Higgins Farm—the barns, the trees, the pond, the endless sunflower fields—had an unnerving ambience to it.

Amy's main problem was the sunflowers. So gorgeous. So iconic, so happy.

So *wrong* . . .

Amy found the sunflowers' scent—or rather, their lack of one—totally weird. The towering plants (which admittedly made fantastic camouflage now) had a strange smell to them—all stalk and leaf and no bloom.

Amy, who loved perfumes as much as the next woman, was puzzled as to where all the gorgeous and fruity Elizabeth Arden fragrance had vanished to. This place smelt nothing like her perfumes.

Walking through this field now, she felt a lot was missing from the vegetal vista surrounding her. Why did these wonderful flowers smell as bland as spinach or lettuce? Even a cornfield smelt better than this. Something was missing, the essence of 'flowerhood' subtracted from the pretty blooms that towered over her.

Not surprisingly then, Amy walked in a strange unease. She already knew a lot was wrong here, but because of these odorless golden blossoms, harmless in their natural innocence, that previously quantifiable trouble now seemed positively mountainous.

***

Maybe it was the flowers, maybe an attempt to ignore the flowers, but for several moments, Amy was distracted. A pleasant memory came to her mind.

She'd not told the guys the full story of her survival. Yes, she'd visited her tent for a quick pick-me-up. But she'd also gone there for some quick flirty sex.

She did this occasionally. Her eye would light on some hunk in the party crowd and she'd just have to have him. Last night had been no different. She'd quickly hooked up with a hot single guy named Johnny Fenton. Their signal to slip away had been when she began playing *Kitten Kitten* by the Ambient Godfathers. The song was about gentle ethereal sex and Amy loved making love to it. She'd put on an extended mix of the track and gone offstage.

The ecstasy she'd taken earlier had her feeling like a kite floating over the dance hall, like the music was resident in her bones. She felt as if her bones were loudspeakers.

Johnny had been waiting for her in the tent. Tall, sexy, dark, gray-eyed. No time to do it slow like the music suggested. She'd quickly unzipped and kicked off her white boots and pulled off her pants. He popped out of his pants too, bone-hard and throbbing with desire for her. She'd kissed him, first on the lips, then on the crown of his swollen manhood, nibbling his bunched-up foreskin before slipping a rubber over it. Then she'd laid on her back on a cot, spread her legs wide, parted her lady-parts and invited his worshipper to come visit her lady temple. He'd filled her gladly, paid intense homage to her wet, tight and waiting womanhood, praising her sexiness with a chorus of gasps and grunts.

The song *Kitten Kitten* played above them, filling her head with its dreamy chords:

"I need you around me,
I really need you around me,
Cos, girl, your kitty astounds me.
You're so soft and silky,
So good for me.
I gotta have you around me, lady,
For today and eternity . . ."

Oh, yes, she'd been all 'around' him, alright. Not just inside her body but outside it too, wrapping him in all four limbs like she was wrapping paper and he was her present for the birthday girl.

It had been over almost immediately for both of them. Barely a minute of synergistic genital motion and they'd both arrived at the orgasmic launching pad. Simultaneous blast off. The penis had felt like a rocket launcher blowing her ass away. Ecstasy in her head, ecstasy in her womanhood. Sexplosions and commingled grunts of physical delight ensued.

He'd sneaked away afterwards, after they'd made a date for later that night.

She'd laid grinning on the cot for a while, then pulled on her white pants again. She'd left her boots off for the moment. No real hurry. The track *Kitten Kitten* still had three minutes to run; she'd time her arrival back on the stage to coincide with the start of *Love The Way You Hate Me* by Bruno Davis Sex Machine. That and some scratching would both lift the party higher and make it seem like she'd planned it that way all along.

But first, now that her body was sated with physical sensation for the moment . . .

She'd pulled out the two baggies—coke and E—and wondered if she dared take some more ecstasy. She decided against it. She didn't want to mess this up. She was the party queen, the fun maker. She never messed up, never gave less than a hundred percent of her talent to her clients.

At the moment, her perceptions enhanced by the E, she was riding the music like a jockey on a horse, totally in control of both herself and the party. She didn't just feel the rhythm, she was the damn rhythm.

But one more tablet, even half of one and she could lose it . . .

She rehydrated with some Sprite instead.

So cocaine it would be then. Just a little snort to even out the edges of her slightly frayed consciousness.

She'd been opening the baggie of white rocket fuel when the music and lights died. A professional to the core, Amy had instantly forgotten about doing the cocaine and slipped both packages into her pockets again.

Then came chaos. The chaos she still inhabited.

More than once since yesterday, she'd wondered if maybe she hadn't actually taken that additional ecstasy tablet . . . only it hadn't been ecstasy at all, but rather a hallucinogen-tainted pill that had fried her mind.

She wondered if this wasn't actually a psychotic interlude she was having now, trapped inside her own head with no way out.

But the crystal-clear knowledge that she'd had five ecstasy pills in her baggie yesterday night and that she still had all five pills on her now was a damning reality check that she'd not OD'd, that she was still in the real world, howbeit in a part of it where strange new laws now applied.

***

While she'd been reminiscing, they'd arrived at the barn.

"Well, here we are," Darrin duly noted.

Amy Fox examined her two companions. Neither man showed any sign that they considered the sunflowers odd at all. Both of them might just as well have been striding through green ruins, or beneath a green mechanical framework.

Ahead of them, the red-eye with the blue reptile burden walked into the barn.

Let's just do this, Amy decided grimly, following the guys towards the barn entrance.

CHAPTER 51

Amy, Darrin & Michael

They crept into the barn after the red-eye.

This was a much longer and larger barn than the others. It had also fallen into disrepair; seemed to have been abandoned for quite a while.

The long building was only lighted at its far end. Once inside its entrance they stood in enforced dusk. A pile of rusted machinery rose on their right, stacked pallets and bales of hay lay to their left, while directly ahead of them, arranged around the barn's central pillars, were stacks of crates and boxes that almost reached the barn roof.

The red-eye dragged its bisected blue burden between the crates and scrap metal, in a straight line for the barn's far right end.

"Alright, where's Ronan?" Darrin whispered, hefting the shotgun.

From where they stood they couldn't see the farmer.

They could hear him though. He sounded hard at work at some activity on the left side of the barn, opposite where the red-eye was headed.

Amy pointed ahead, to the right, where the red-eye had just dumped its burden of bleeding blue meat on top of a workbench.

"Okay," she whispered, "so now we've confirmed that that's the only red-eye left. We need a plan of action."

Michael had his phone out and was recording everything. "We already have one. We find our wives, get evidence, then get the hell out of here."

Amy nodded. "Yeah, but *where are* your wives? Or, for that matter, all the corpses that were brought in here yesterday? There isn't anyone in here."

This was true. As far as they could see, not a soul was in sight.

Its burden disposed of, the red-eye was now standing motionless in a corner.

"It's waiting for instructions," Amy pointed out. "It's not a threat to us until Ronan or Cathy orders it to attack us."

"So we need take out Ronan and Cathy first," Darren said. "Come on, let's go get Ronan, he's somewhere over there on the left, behind those crates."

They moved farther into the barn, the gloom lightening as they went.

As they stepped forward, a sickening reek of raw meat hit them. The smell was nauseating, as if someone had recently butchered a herd of cows or sheep in here and not bothered to clean up afterward. The smell of spilled blood and body fluids was thick in the air, intensifying as they neared the crates. Something also smelt burnt, as if a few of the crates had earlier caught fire but had been put out.

"Guys, that workbench near the red-eye is covered with something red," Michael noted as he swept his phone camera right. "Looks like blood to me."

"Go, go!" Amy urged.

Darrin in front, they ran past the crates.

They took cover behind some ancient bales of hay that reeked of mold.

They peeked out at Ronan. They were fifteen feet away from him.

"What the fuck?" Amy and Michael both gasped, at the same time but for entirely different reasons.

***

Amy:

Ahead of them, Ronan, his pants down around his ankles, was having sex with someone—no, with some*thing*. His sexual partner, who was bent over stacked pallets, would have been human except for the size and color of her head.

'She' was naked. They could see that her body was perfectly normal and female, but her head . . .

Her head was four times normal-sized, a blotchy light/dark blue in color, and had eyes the size of motorbike headlamps. As Ronan's hips thrust her back and forth, a yellow goo spilled from her ridiculously small mouth. Between squirts of goo, she let out small yelps that could have been cries of either pleasure or pain.

"That's . . . that's . .. that's Sylvia!" Amy gasped in horror.

Darrin turned to gape at her. "Sylvia? How the hell can that be Sylvia?"

Amy was shaking now. "Look at her arm. The tattoo. The tattoo."

Darrin nodded and looked. Sure enough, on her left upper arm, Ronan's crazily misshaped partner had Sylvia Stewart's red-and-yellow tattoo of a butterfly with 'Love Bug' written in blue across its wings.

Darrin stared, wiped his eyes in disbelief, then stared some more. Focused on his sex act, oblivious to their presence and grunting loudly, Ronan continued to relentlessly sodomize Sylvia with a freakishly large erection. Darrin now noticed (just like Amy already had), that Ronan had two red horns growing from his forehead, and that no, what he'd earlier thought a trick of the light wasn't that at all—Ronan actually *was* blue all over.

He gaped at Amy again. "What's going on here?"

"C'mon, man, gimme a break," she groaned back in acute mental distress. "How'm I supposed to know that? We both arrived here together." She was fighting to get her shakes under control and just about succeeding. She looked like she'd prefer to be screaming though, just that she realized that if she did so the resulting exposure would be really bad for all of them.

***

Michael:

"Guys, you gotta look at this," he whispered hoarsely. Then, when neither Amy nor Darrin paid him any attention because of the crazy sex spectacle ahead of them, he kicked Amy's foot. "Hey, look over *here,* both of you. I'm about going crazy."

That was when the others turned and saw the plants too, and instantly forgot the perplexing question of how Sylvia Stewart had been transformed from the beautiful woman they'd known into the circus freak Ronan was copulating with; and also the question of why Ronan Higgins now looked like a demon, or at least a nightmare version of the Disney genie from *Aladdin.*

"What is this?" Darrin whispered. "What is going on here?"

"Man, if I could answer that . . ."

Amy just stared. She had no words. None at all.

To the right of the three of them stood sixteen of the craziest plants they'd ever seen. Each was seven or eight feet high, black as coal, and had tentacles instead of leaves. The only reason they knew the things were plants at all was because they were planted in metal tubs, tubs stained with blood. At the bottom of the nearest tub they saw roots that looked like black hands.

They could also see clearly why the tubs were stained with blood: each of them contained a varying amount of raw meat. Some were half-full, others almost overflowed with hacked-up flesh. Every few moment, the black plants scooped the meat up silently and popped it into their mouths.

Mouths? Yes, this was the craziest detail of all: the plants all had faces at the base of their trunks, below the start of their tentacles. Human faces. Some of them had two or three faces, stacked on each other as if the plant was a demonic totem pole. All with horribly realistic features that moved in a parody of human expression. All with teeth like rows of yellow nails.

Amy, Michael and Darrin stared, horror slowly cutting through their disbelief.

CHAPTER 52

Friends, Drugs & Rock 'N' Roll . . .

Michael, who'd first noticed the plants, had a head start on his companions in the recovery stakes. "That's human flesh they're eating," he whispered. "See, that's blonde hair on the chunk this one's putting into its mouth. And that's . . . that's someone's breasts."

"And there goes a foot down a gullet," Darrin added. His face was white. He gripped the Remington 870 as if he was trying to break the shotgun in two.

"Guys, that ain't even close to the worst of it," Amy said, finally finding her voice.

"What could possibly be worse than this shit?"

Amy delivered the bad news in a flat voice. "You guys, look at the *faces* on the plants—if they *are* plants—recognize anyone?"

And that was when the others saw it too—saw that each of the black tentacled plants had the face of at least one of their friends. Some had the faces of two or three of their close friends. Faces of people they recognized. People who had been at yesterday's party. Darrin recognized Tommy Ashton, Ann Bosworth, Jerry and Tammy Coombs, Sylvia's boyfriend Barry McCain, Annie and Tony Haggerty, Mark Jacobson and several others.

"He chopped them all up and fed them to his plants and the plants absorbed them and . . ." Amy's voice trailed off in disgust. She'd been thinking aloud, and like her voice, her thoughts had just run themselves out of steam from the sheer insanity of the concepts she was considering. This wasn't possible. It just wasn't possible. But here it was, the whole nightmare scenario occurring right in front of her and daring her to refute its existence: the black trees scooping up bleeding human meat in their tentacles to feed themselves, to feed each 'friend face's' mouth what might even be their own corpse-flesh.

Who on earth had thought this up?

Not on Earth, Amy, the knowledge popped into her mind. *No one on Earth is evil enough to conceive something like this. Something as mad as this came from a realm where insanity is considered logical, where madness has its own appeal and receives acclaim, receives praise because everyone there is insane too.*

And then Michael, who was still video recording, spotted Sharon's face. He'd been praying that she'd escaped this outrage. But she hadn't . . . no she hadn't.

His eyes clouded over with rage. "I'm gonna kill that bastard," he growled.

"We both are," Darrin said quietly, his eyes filling with tears. "I can't see Vanni anywhere on this side. Most likely she's on the other side of the plants."

Amy watched them. Two men who'd just lost their wives to a nightmare. She wondered how they'd cope. Darrin just seemed sad and lost. But Michael? The rage in Michael's gaze was terrifying in its intensity. He'd stopped filming now, was holding his phone like it was a gun. For a moment she thought he was going to leap up out of concealment and charge Ronan and try to hack his head off with the axe in his other hand.

But Michael didn't, though he was clearly exerting a massive amount of effort to bring himself under control.

And then, when he calmed down, he said the strangest thing to Darrin: "Aw shit, man, I guess this son-of-a-bitch did help us resolve our dilemma."

Darrin stared at him coldly. "What dilemma?"

Michael laughed mirthlessly. "How to tell the girls that we'd made porno stars of 'em." He gestured at Ronan's weird plants. "The thought of having to do that scared me way more than these goddam hell-trees do."

Amy, of course, didn't know what he meant. Nor did she believe him. Watching the black plants sweep up her friend's chopped remains in their bloody tentacles and feed themselves made her feel like running away screaming while simultaneously pissing and shitting herself. And they still had the creepy-looking Ronan to deal with. Nothing could be more scary than that combination.

But Amy was a fighter; she was staying to see this whole damn thing through. Even though . . . even though she'd just noticed the face of her last night's beau—Johnny Fenton—over on the far side of the plants, a blood-slick cord of intestines dangling from its lips. She quickly looked away from the nauseating sight. She forced all memories of the dead man from her mind; it was either that or succumb to the mania she felt encroaching on her mental space. She concentrated on swallowing her terror and being as brave as she could.

Darrin dried his eyes with the back of his hand. He smiled too now, though his eyes were like chips of prehistoric flint. "Yeah, Mike, the bastard sure did, didn't he? But we're still gonna kill his ass, aren't we?"

They turned from the demonic plants back to their demonic planter.

Michael put his cellphone away. "Yeah, dude, we definitely are gonna kill Ronan. Firstly, because he killed our wives who we loved with all our hearts. And secondly, so that he goddamn stops making all that irritating sexual racket. Shit!—doesn't the asshole ever come? Or is Sylvia's ass that damn slack?"

Amy had been wondering about that too. Ronan had been loudly humping away on the transformed Sylvia since they'd arrived. Now, peeking over the top of the stacked bales of hay, they saw he was still going hard at it, gripping the woman's knees and lifting her legs off the floor so she was lying flat on the pallet, while she endlessly drooled and flailed like she was in mortal agony. It was hard to tell though if she was actually suffering. With that massive blue head of hers— which Amy honestly thought looked like a globe of the Earth where everything was ocean—slobbering yellow goo everywhere, she might just as well be in ecstasy. In this impossible scenario, anything was possible.

"Okay, what's the plan?" Amy whispered, shaking her gun.

"First of all," Darrin replied, "you still got those drugs on you? I mean, the coke?"

She nodded.

"Let's have it. I think I need some Colombian courage right now."

She looked at Michael. He nodded.

She brought out the baggie, then spilt a little hill of the white powder on the back of each of their hands. She made a little pile for herself too, then secured the rest in her jeans again.

They each snorted it up. No danger of being heard. Ronan and Sylvia were still making a hell of a sexual ruckus. Ronan was grunting now like he'd come soon.

"We're here to do drugs and kill monsters," Amy said.

"What?"

"I meant—to do drugs and kill demons." She grinned, the coke exploding like bombs in her head. "Ignore me—I'm just gearing myself up for the fight ahead." Then she sobered a little, though her eyes gleamed. "Alright, like I was saying: the plan?"

"What you got in mind?"

She pointed right, her thoughts a little haphazard but sharper too. She felt greatly intensified. "The red-eye is over there. It's no threat yet and Cathy hasn't yet shown up either. So we can . . ." A cunning look entered her eyes. "Hey, to be on the safe side, shouldn't we just shoot him from here and have done with it?"

"A shotgun blast might splatter Sylvia to hell too," Darrin objected.

"The way she looks now, I think she'll be thankful to be splattered," Amy said. "I can't see her ever going out in public again looking like that."

Now the sight of Sylvia was making Amy queasy, filling her with an urge to vomit that the plants hadn't achieved. She didn't know if it was the coke or whatever, but also she felt marginally unstable.

Her companions, though, looked none the worse for wear. She suspected that in their cases, the cocaine high had temporarily neutralized the downer of losing their wives. And what was that story of turning their wives into porno actresses? Was she hearing things now or what?

"I really don't see that it matters if we hit Sylvia," she insisted in a rushed whisper.

"No," Michael said. "What she's got might be curable."

"If she's curable, then I'm Ivanka Trump."

"Whatever. We *aren't* shooting her."

Amy shrugged. "Oh, alright—she still has my party balance to pay me anyway; though I don't see the bank ever confirming her identity with her looking like that. Okay, how about if I just shoot *him* then? I can easily blow his brains out from here."

Michael regarded her with some suspicion. "You sure?"

"As sure as I'm sure that if you have sex with me just once, you'll instantly divorce your already dead wife and marry me instead."

At her irreverent comment, Michael's mouth twisted up like he'd eaten something bitter. She saw it, but didn't care. And anyway, she figured it was true: she *was* great at making love. In a man's bed, there were few women she couldn't give a lifelong run for their money.

Just that at the moment, sex wasn't the business at hand.

"Okay," Michael grunted. "You take care of him."

She looked at Darrin, who nodded back at her.

Ronan was bent down low now over Sylvia and humping hard to reach his climax. Amy aimed the Sig Sauer P220 at Ronan's head. But that meant she was looking at his red horns. The horns distracted her. She couldn't get his horns out of her mind. Six inches long, each of them; red and thick as a guy's penis.

And speaking of penises . . .

Just as she was about pulling the trigger, Ronan finally ejaculated.

She got the shot off, but saw it go wide as Ronan suddenly jerked upright due to his orgasm. Before she could aim and fire again, Ronan, alerted by the gunshot noise, pulled out of Sylvia.

The farmer turned, saw Amy and the two men, and howled, "Get them!"

"He just called for the red-eye," Michael said. "Amy, shoot him again!"

But Amy couldn't. And not because she was scared. She was simply nauseated. On withdrawing his mutated erection from his niece's buttocks, Ronan had left a gaping hole between them. The anus was so distended now, it seemed large enough for Amy to fit an entire foot into. In addition, the fiendishly dilated anus was streaming with lumpy blue semen, as if Sylvia's rectum was an uncorked jam jar.

The sight was too much for Amy's stomach. She turned and began retching, the puke coming hard and fast.

Shit, shit shit shit shit! she thought while vomiting. Only there wasn't any feces in that gaping chasm of an ass hole, just blue jelly mix.

Ronan meanwhile, hastily packed his penis away and ducked out of sight behind the tentacled plants. He left 'Sylvia' lying there stretched out over the pallets, limp like she was dead, and with that nasty mess leaking out of her backside as if she was hemorrhaging azure blood. Her giant blue head looked like a mutant watermelon that someone had shoved her actual head into.

Michael and Darrin had meanwhile burst into action.

"Stay here and keep watch for Cathy," Darrin whispered to Amy as they hurried past her. "Yeah, and alert us if that ten-foot-tall guy suddenly returns. We want to have a word with him."

"Or run the hell away from him," Michael added.

Amy was glad to play sentry. She felt terrible.

Maybe snorting that coke under these circumstances wasn't such a hot idea after all, she thought, wincing as the Bolivian shooting stars in her head all fell to Earth like meteorite rain, and the dust of their explosions further upset her already unsettled belly.

CHAPTER 53

Michael & Darrin

Remington 870 in Darrin's hands, axe and a bottle of water in Michael's, both men ran past Ronan's plants. They avoided looking at the black plants. They didn't want to see the faces on them again. They could hear the hellish foliage greedily feeding. Twice, hungry tentacles reached out and tried to grab them. But they forced themselves not to look at the horrible things. They kept their distance from the evil plants and safely passed along the wall of crates to the barn's other side.

Over there as they'd expected, the red-eye was coming towards them, arms outstretched as if preparing for a welcoming hug. Its hands were on fire. A visible mist rose from it as its black body shimmered with impossible heat. Its eyes glared as if its brain was a bonfire inside its otherwise featureless head.

For a moment, the sight of the glittering black creature struck intense fear into Michael. But then thoughts of Sharon flashed through his mind. He imagined the pain she'd felt dying. His mind shed its dread. It refilled up with hatred instead.

He grinned coldly at the hell-thing. "Hey, dude, you like, really need to cool off, you know. Here, have some water."

He flung the bottle of water at the red-eye.

The red-eye caught the bottle of water in midair, which was its undoing. The heat of its flaming fingers immediately melted the plastic. The water splattered back over its head and shoulders, and that was its end. There was a mighty 'Kaboom!' and then pieces of the creature were strewn everywhere around Michael and Darrin like chunks of smoking anthracite. A piece of it had even blown out a nearby window. It was a minor miracle that no part of the exploding creature had hit them.

The red-eye's legs lay near the plant tubs, sizzling and blowing off clouds of steam like they were sauna rocks. Its two-toed feet still twitched, slowly flexing down to standstill. Half of the creature's torso was over by the barn wall, flinging off red sparks like a whirling whetstone and glowing like the interior of a blacksmith's crucible.

Michael looked down. There was a tiny chunk of red-eye by his left foot. Without thinking, he bent to pick it up.

Next moment he howled in pain and dropped it again. "Dammit! It's hotter than grabbing a soldering iron by the tip!" He stuck his thumb and forefinger in his mouth and began sucking on them.

"You alright, dude?" Darrin asked.

Michael kept on sucking his smarting fingers. "I just need a minute," he growled in pain.

Darrin waved the shotgun at Ronan's tentacled plants. "Now, where to find their daddy?"

Then he froze. "Aw, shit . . ."

He pointed forward along the few remaining yards to the end of the barn. Words were unnecessary. Michael had seen it too. The corpse-meat pile.

Though now greatly reduced in size due to the hell-plants' regular feedings, there was still enough meat piled there on the barn floor to make up at least six people: bits of legs and arms and torsos (lots of shattered ribs and vertebrae and lung chunks), pieces of heads, feet and hands (both complete and split into fingers and toes); and guts, seemingly miles of guts.

Mingled in with the pervasive stench of death was a subtle hint of roasting, which only made everything the more horrible, as if they stood inside the Devil's kitchen.

Beside the workbench stood the axe that had created this vista of human deconstruction; its haft and blade liberally coated with human gore. Beyond the workbench, a chainsaw sat on a wood stump, but this had a clean gleaming blade. So the axe had been Ronan's tool of choice, wielded with lunatic purpose to achieve a maniacal effect.

All around them, all over the floor they stood on, was spilled blood.

They were standing in an ocean of blood. A literal ocean of carnage.

Up until this moment, it hadn't really struck either man how much violence had occurred in this barn, on this farm. But now, faced with the damning evidence—piled slightly-burnt clothes and shoes, a smaller pile of men's wallets and women's purses, and finally, that horrifying mess of chopped meat that had once been people they knew, people who even now seemed to be eating 'themselves' from their new plant posts—both men felt almost paralyzed by terror.

No, this was beyond mere terror. Both men felt overwhelmed by the sheer scale of this bizarre evil. Shotgun and axe trembled in Darrin and Michael's respective grasps; two brave men ready for action but scared that even these deadly weapons they bore would prove less than adequate against what they were facing here.

Dismayed, they turned from staring at the human remains to staring at the plants that were feeding on them. Then they stared at the bloody workbench, where that also inexplicable mottled-blue lizard half-carcass lay, looking for all the world like something from outer space, though it also reminded them both of the strange transformation that had happened to Sylvia's head—it had something weirdly 'human' about its massive feet.

"Where the hell is Ronan?" Darrin finally spat in an intenseness of disgust that transcended both loss and fear. "I daresay he's got a lot of explaining to do.

CHAPTER 54

Sylvia's Pleasure

Sylvia was in ecstasy.

At first she'd been in utter agony from the nails in her hands and the knowledge that her uncle was raping her.

But suddenly, everything had changed. Once swallowed, Ronan's blue demon semen had had the effect of an aphrodisiac on Sylvia.

Now everything was pure pleasure.

She had no idea of her physical transformation. No idea that she now looked like a circus freak with a blue head bigger than a beach ball, or that her eyes were both the color and size of ripe grapefruit.

All she knew now was the pleasure. The come had turned her on, and her mind was spinning and well out of control. Her rectum throbbed with emptiness and want. She wanted more penis inside her body, more orgasms that felt like she was living forever.

Sylvia looked down at her hands, and then at her feet. All the nail holes dripped with sticky blue liquid. It was all very pretty and felt good. Her legs too were covered with blue liquid. She was standing in it.

Sylvia picked herself up from the pallets. The blue man responsible for her pleasure was somewhere nearby. Why had he abandoned her? She didn't understand it. She wanted him. She needed him. More pleasure! More pleasure! More! More! More!

Supporting her massive head in her hands so it didn't overbalance her, she staggered away from her pallet bed. As her luminous eyes searched the barn, desperation rose in her heart.

She had to find the blue-skinned man. Was he hiding from her? Why would he do that? Didn't he know that she needed him more than she needed life itself?

She looked forward. There was a woman a short distance in front of her.

"Psst, Sylvia!" the woman was saying. "It's me, Amy Fox!"

But Sylvia didn't know her. And even if she did, *she* wasn't important now. She wasn't *him*, her magic man. He alone held the key to the pleasure she desired to keep flooding her—the orgasms, the endless orgasms . . .

"Sylvia! Over here!"

She ignored the woman. She turned away, back towards the pallets. Maybe her lover was hiding on the other side of the black plants . . .

But in her ecstatic stupor, Sylvia had strayed too close to the plants. In a flash, several of them flung out tentacles and snared her.

"No!" the other woman gasped behind her. "No, no, no, no, no!"

As she was yanked away into the midst of the plants, Sylvia caught a glimpse of the woman. She wondered why she looked so terrified, why she had her fingers pressed tightly to her mouth and was trembling with fright.

While Sylvia made weak moves of resistance, the plants began tearing her apart and eating her, biting off mouthfuls of her flesh with those teeth of theirs like yellow six-inch nails. Ravenous gluttons, they pulled off her limbs, then further split those limbs apart and shoved them into their many mouths. They messily mined her diverse organs, penetrated her orifices and shredded and extracted her bowels.

Sylvia's guts they spread between themselves like purple washing line and began tugging on as if playing one of those string games where a string loop is continually rearranged by the fingers of both hands.

And so Sylvia Stewart died. Died very messily. But the odd thing about this was, the ecstasy never left Sylvia till her very last breath. Sylvia felt her strange death as the most intense orgasm ever.

It really was a beautiful death.

CHAPTER 55

Amy

Amy was riveted to the spot by what she was witnessing. The most horrible part of it for her was when the plants broke open Sylvia's enlarged head—they simply pulled it apart like it was a rotten pumpkin—and began fishing inside it for her brains.

Seeing that, Amy had to resist the strong urge to puke again.

It was while the hell-plants were harvesting the pink spongy mass that filled Sylvia's head that Amy realized she wasn't alone anymore.

She spun around. However, doing so merely helped her face connect better with the two-by-four being swung at it.

Turning around also let her see that it was Cathy Higgins who'd just knocked her out.

CHAPTER 56

Michael & Darrin

"So, where the hell did he vanish to?" Michael asked. They'd heard some agitation and excitement on the other side of the plants, but couldn't attend to that now.

Darrin peered among the feeding hell-plants, their constantly moving tentacles obscuring his vision. "He ain't hiding in there. So . . ."

"WATCH OUT!" Michael yelled next.

Too late. Ronan had already plunged the pitchfork through Darrin's body.

The demonic farmer had appeared suddenly from behind some corrugated aluminum sheets leaning against the wall. He'd come out fast as a bullet.

Now, he forced Darrin's pierced and bleeding body forward, ramming him into Michael, making Michael slip on the bloody-slick floor.

Fighting not to fall, Michael skidded back, losing his axe along the way.

Darrin had already dropped his shotgun. Now his hands gripped the prongs of the pitchfork, trying to free himself from them. This was impossible while Ronan was shoving the pitchfork deeper through him from behind. Darrin stood there gaping at Michael while blood streamed from his belly and mouth.

Michael spotted the Remington a distance behind Ronan. He dashed to pick it up. But Cathy suddenly appeared from somewhere and reached the shotgun first.

"Back off," she said, covering Michael with the weapon. "Trust me, I know how to use this."

She was smiling like she was eager to use it too. Michael backed off. Just like her father, Cathy was blue all over now and had red horns too. Her skin was weird, like she had navy blue eczema. She also had a raw wound on her throat, a deep and puckered slit that appeared to circle all around her neck.

Ronan nodded at Cathy. "Where's the girl? The DJ?"

Cathy jerked her head sideways. "Getting her beauty sleep and waiting for Prince Charming to show up and kiss her awake again. According to the fairy tale, that usually takes ninety-nine years to happen though."

Ronan nodded his approval. "That's my girl."

Ronan shoved the pitchfork forward and let go of it, so Darrin fell flat on his face. The force of his impact with the floor knocked the pitchfork prongs out of his body. Ronan picked the fork up and flung it aside.

Michael knelt and rolled Darrin over, then sat him up. Darrin was still alive, but spitting blood. He was covered with muck but breathing regularly, if weakly.

"Take it easy, man," Michael whispered. "We'll still get out of this somehow. I, for one, have got a kid to get back home to."

Darrin nodded. "Yeah, and we'll both marry hot new wives and they'll fuck each other too and we'll make porno actresses out of them too. Doesn't seem worth it, bro."

"No? C'mon, man, think of all the money you'll make," Michael was talking just to keep Darrin conscious. It didn't matter what he said, sense or nonsense, just so long as his best friend didn't shut his eyes never to reopen them again. "Or, if you're so worried about the wives cheating on us, we won't get married again. We'll just stay single and run our porno empire as bachelors."

Darrin laughed, a lot of blood spilling over his lower lip and dribbling down his chin. "Yeah, I could live that decadent lifestyle." He made a weak sweeping gesture. "Hot babes everywhere . . ."

"Yeah, just stay alive. Don't die on me now, man."

"Yeah, dude, we're gonna shoot loadsa porn and have lotsa fun and sex and—"

Michael caught a flash of motion out of the corner of his eye and ducked out of the way.

He'd moved just in time. Swung by Ronan, the axe hit Darrin square in the middle of his head. It split Darrin's skull completely in two, spilling brains everywhere, before ploughing on down through his neck also and burying its blade deep inside his chest.

Michael leapt up and stared. Darrin's cleaved body was jerking and erupting blood, left, right and center.

Ronan retrieved the axe from Darrin's corpse. "That's what you get for lying to me, asshole. I knew my eyes weren't deceiving me. Your wife and his wife *were* Candy Richmond and Mandy Paris."

Michael gaped at him. "What? You killed him for that?"

"Just joking," the farmer coldly replied. "And I'm gonna kill you too. But, trust me, dying's alright. There's loads of gorgeous succubae in Hell who'll be delighted to star in any pornos you two got in mind after I dispatch you down there."

Michael thought hard and fast, wondering how to escape this nightmare predicament. But Cathy had him well covered with the shotgun.

CHAPTER 57

Ensemble of Death

"I really like you," Cathy told Michael. "Come on, let's make love. My dad won't mind; he's real easygoing."

Michael looked at the girl, trying to make sense of what she'd just said. Have sex with her? Darrin was lying next to him in a pool of blood, cut almost in two, fluffy chunks of his brain spilled from his head like wet popcorn, and she wanted to 'make love' with him?

She waved the shotgun at him, her blue face intense. "Come on, don't be shy. I mean it, dad honestly won't mind if we go off and do it." She frowned thoughtfully. "I don't understand it myself, but since coming back from the dead, I've been as horny as . . . it feels like I've a fire burning between my legs all the time, like something's crawling in my womb which can only be satisfied by a man."

"Cut that pubic nonsense out!" Ronan growled at her. "We ain't got time for that. We've work to do."

"O-kay." She wagged the shotgun in Michael's direction. "Can I keep him for later then?"

"No, he's evidence. He's got to be killed too. Bargainer's orders."

Cathy pouted. She looked like she'd protest, but then said, "Oh alright, dad, if you say so. Hey, dad, shouldn't Uncle Bargainer be back yet? He might like to meet Michael."

Ronan shrugged. "The Bargainer's a busy man, Cathy. He's got lots of deals to make, both here and on the Static Earth. He can't be everywhere at once. He'll arrive in due time."

She gestured at Michael. "Should I shoot him now?"

"Yeah. Might as well chop them both up with the other meat in the pile and have done with it."

Michael stared at the pair in horror. "Why?" He asked Ronan. "Why are you doing this?"

Ronan sighed. "It's the deal, see. I dunno what the Bargainer wants with these carnivorous plants I'm growing for him. All I know is that growing 'em brought my daughter back to life and is keeping her alive still."

Michael shook his head in disbelief. "Dead? Are you blind, man? She's still alive!"

Ronan shook his head too. "You don't get it, city boy. Cathy here died. But the Bargainer brought her back to me. And for good, this time. According to the Bargainer, neither of us are ever gonna die again."

To demonstrate this, he pulled out a knife from his jeans and sliced his arm open. The revealed flesh was blue and dripped purple blood.

Michael's eyes widened as the wound instantly sealed itself again.

Ronan nodded. "Like I said: Cathy and me are both immortal now. We can't ever be killed. We're gonna live forever."

"Looking like this?" Michael couldn't help the question. How did the pair of them expect to fit into society with blue skin and red horns?

"Uncle Bargainer is taking us both back with him to the Static Earth," Cathy informed Michael. "And there—like my dad says— we'll both live forever."

"Unlike you, city boy," Ronan said, "who's about to go and start making that porno of yours in Hell along with your friend." He smirked, running a finger along his right horn. "Well, it's been nice knowing you, Michael, but, like they say—all bad things gotta happen sooner or later." He turned to his daughter. "Cathy, fetch the chainsaw, I feel like getting my hands really wet and dirty with this one."

What? Chainsaw? Michael made his move then, darting right, behind the workbench. He slipped once, righted himself, and made it around the long wooden table.

But then he was faced with the corpse pile.

He was scrambling over the hill of torn flesh and intestines when Ronan rammed into him like an NFL linebacker.

Michael slammed into the barn wall and blacked out.

***

What woke Michael up again was a shot of agonizing pain in his belly.

He jerked upright to the atrocious sight of Ronan yanking his intestines out of his body in wet handfuls. He was up on the workbench now and had been stripped naked and his belly cut open while he was unconscious. The front of his abdomen lay spread in two bleeding halves, with his guts extending from the hole like a length of rope that Ronan was reeling in.

Somewhere nearby Michael could hear a loud strident noise like someone had angered a giant nest of bees.

"Noooooo!" he screamed at the sight of himself opened up like an autopsy.

Ronan laughed. "Don't worry 'bout it, city boy. It'll be over soon."

Michael shoved Ronan away from him. He tried getting up and managed to sit. As he did so, his guts spilled out en masse.

Ronan got out of the way. Cathy stepped forward with the whirling chainsaw and stuck it deep into the bloody hole in Michael's body. After butchering his liver, she angled the chainsaw up, so it reached his lungs and heart.

Ronan hadn't lied. It was soon over. But still, Michael died in incredible pain.

CHAPTER 58

Amy

Amy woke up, her head ringing like she was the White House buzzer and all the world presidents were fighting to get into the building to confront Donald Trump over some trade agreement that didn't favor them.

She sat up groggily and felt her left temple. The skin was broken. Her fingers came away wet with blood.

Damn that Cathy!

Amy suddenly realized that part of the buzzing she was hearing was actually outside of her head. It was the sound of a chainsaw coming from across the barn, beyond the patch of black plants.

She heard voices. Ronan speaking; now and then Cathy too. The voices were indistinct. This was mostly because of the chainsaw, but also partly because of Amy's throbbing head, and partly because of the hell-plants' rustling noises as they ate their meals of shredded human flesh. The plant sounds existed on the verge of Amy's consciousness, soft as the wind and evil as sin; the horror of their meaning a distraction to clear thought.

Amy stared groggily at the monstrous plants, trying to find even a glimmer of self-awareness in the eyes of their many faces. There was none, each familiar visage was now merely an extension of its host plant, the means by which the fat black trunk fed itself, and possibly by which it viewed the world also. The plants didn't seem intelligent, but one could never tell. The way they'd grabbed Sylvia proved they were aware of their environment, if not of themselves.

All that remained of Sylvia now was some brunette hair on the barn floor. Amy made a mental note to stay well away from the plants.

The chainsaw noise cut out then. She heard Ronan say: "Well, that's those two taken care of. Let's chop 'em up then fetch the DJ girl."

She felt shock and fear. *Michael and Darrin are both dead? And they plan to kill me next?*

"Ha ha ha," Cathy laughed. "I'm sure they both wish they were immortal like us now."

"Roll that swollen blue thing off the table. No, I better chop it up too. What it that anyway?"

"A guy named Ben. I met him last night. We dated for nine hours, but then he swelled up badly and died."

"He blew up?"

"No, dad—he didn't explode."

"How'd he die then, girl? The red-eyes get him?"

"No, he—"

Amy lost both the girl's reply and some later conversation between father and daughter amidst nasty chopping and squelchy noises that continued for awhile, punctuated with laughter and giggling.

Then, in the morbid silence after a rapid-fire burst of chopping block noises that had sounded like an elementary school class having their heads cut off, Ronan said: "Sad. I'd really have liked to *meat* him . . . get it, Cathy—*meat* him?"

"Ha ha ha! Dad, you're so funny. But . . . Oh, I miss him so much."

"Now, don't you start crying, girl. First love's always like that. Come here, give your daddy a hug. You'll get over it, you'll see. Hey, I forgot about your cousin. Where's Sylvia? She hasn't escaped, has she?"

"The plants ate her. I got here too late to prevent it."

"Aw, well. That solves that problem, I guess. At least *we* didn't kill her. We couldn't do that—she was family."

"Yeah, dad, she was."

"Well, I better finish chopping up this Ben of yours too."

Loud axe poundings filled the air.

Amy got to her feet. It was time to move, or else she'd surely share her companions' fate. But she was in bad shape. Her head still throbbed; her muscles felt uncoordinated; her eyes kept losing focus.

To clear her mind, she got the rest of the cocaine out of her pocket, spilled it on the back of her hand and snorted it all up.

She waited till the fireworks in her head had dulled a little. Doing drugs now wasn't really advisable, but it was either that or collapse back on the floor the way Cathy had left her. Now her eyes were clear again, and her brain felt sharper. She could ignore the headache. Heaven knew how long this high would last though.

"It had better last long enough," she muttered to herself. "I've got some big scores to settle with those two, if only because of my stolen record collection. Shit, KC personally autographed that copy of *That's The Way (I Like It)* for me."

Once she felt closer to fine, she looked around for her gun.

If Cathy took it . . .

Yes, Cathy had taken the Sig P220. Amy searched around desperately for a substitute weapon. She saw no axes, adzes or saws. Cathy's two-by-four lay there by her feet, but she doubted it would be much use.

Finally, she found a rusty old sickle wedged between two bales of hay. She worked it free.

This'll have to do. For now.

Sickle in hand, Amy made her way forward around the hell-plants. They reached for her with their thick black tentacles. She kept well away from them.

CHAPTER 59

Ronan, Cathy . . . Amy

Ben's remains joined the meat pile. Ronan dropped the axe. Now he gestured around the barn.

"Cleaning up this mess is gonna be one hell of a job," he said. "It'll take us forever."

Cathy nodded. "Good thing we're gonna live forever then. Means we got all the time in the world to clean the barn up."

They both laughed at that, then Ronan asked: "Hey, girl, what happened to your neck?"

"My head got cut off, but I'm fine now."

"You need to be careful; it ain't fully healed yet."

"Dad, I said I'm fine. Let it be."

"Alright."

'So, dad—what now?'

"Let's go fetch that DJ chick and get this over with. I could do with some rest from all this chopping people up."

"Yeah. But you can't rest yet, we still gotta go find—Hey, what's tha—?"

To a lighting flash of steel, Cathy's head went spinning away off her shoulders again.

Ronan spun around. Amy stepped quickly aside to where Cathy had left the shotgun. She dropped the sickle and picked up the Remington 870.

Ignoring her intrusion for a moment, Ronan looked around for his daughter's head.

Purple 'blood' bubbling from its neck, Cathy's headless body was still slumping to the floor. Her detached head had landed on the meat pile. It faced outwards and was positioned almost upright while half wedged into the remnants of someone's ribcage. From the ribcage's

178

wet state, it likely belonged to either of the just-deceased Michael and Darrin. A loop of intestine that had snagged on Cathy's right horn was helping keep her head in place.

"Dammit," she groaned. "Not again. I gotta stop losing my head in situations like this."

Ronan turned from staring at her to staring at Amy instead.

"You . . . you . . . you . . ." he sputtered, his eyes filled with rage. He stepped towards her. "How dare you? That kid means the world to me."

Amy shrugged without fear.

"Hey, asshole and daughter asshole," she said coldly, "please permit me to reintroduce myself. My name is DJ Amy Fox and I'm a total badass bitch. Now usually, I love to rock a party and help the party animals have a good time." She sniffed, then wiped her nose with the back of her hand. "But today I'm here to do drugs and kill demons." She gestured with the shotgun barrel from Ronan to Cathy's head. "Which, in case you don't get it yet, means you two."

Ronan came at her. She fired. The blast flung Ronan back and down on the bloody floor, but he got up and came at her again, the hole in his belly already closing over.

He smiled evilly. "Maybe you weren't listening earlier, you stupid bitch, but we *can't* be killed. Cathy and I are immortal now—you cut her head off and we simply stick it back on again and it heals and she's perfect again. That's what immortal means. Or do all those narcotics you're on make the English language hard to understand?"

Amy smiled back. The son-of-a-bitch had no idea what she had in store for him. She cocked the Remington and fired again, this time kneeling, so the blast knocked Ronan off his feet and lifted him through the air, then slammed him down like a dropped sack of flour.

"I'm gonna rip your head off, you—!" But then he realized what she'd done. The force of the shotgun blast had flung him right up against his demon plants. Before he could scramble away, the plants had snared him in their black tentacles and were pulling him into their shadowy midst.

"No!" Ronan gasped as they dragged him inward.

Amy smiled sweetly at him. "Sure you can't be killed, baby. But you definitely *can* be eaten." She waved. "Bye, Ronan. Have fun digesting forever."

"NOOOOOOOO!"

That was it for Ronan. Like they'd done with his niece, the plants quickly stripped him of his clothes and skin and flesh, tore him to shreds, partitioned his organs and wolfed down those parts. They shredded him like pizza visiting a frat house, like breakfast cereal that had mistakenly attended a kindergarten class.

Unlike with Sylvia, however, who'd died gasping in ecstasy, Ronan expired screaming in intense and unfeigned agony, while his blood squirted everywhere in purple jets.

Amy watched him vanish. The coke had her stabilized now, sharp as a razor. But she knew cocaine also made one overconfident. Like now.

She almost paid for her high.

She heard shuffling sounds behind her and turned. Axe gripped in both hands, Cathy's headless body was coming at her. She ducked just in time—the axe just missed taking her head off and cut her arm instead.

Wincing from the pain, Amy stared over at Cathy's severed head.

Cathy's eyes were narrowed with concentration. She was willing her body to turn, willing it to raise the axe again. She was totally focused on moving her body in the right direction, mobilizing it to attack Amy. Her body stepped towards Amy. Amy got out of its way.

Then Amy cocked the Remington and walked over towards the meat pile.

"Don't you ever learn, kiddo?"

"You're gonna die! You're gonna die for killing my dad!" Cathy replied angrily. At her words, her body began running at Amy, axe held high to chop her.

Amy once more got out of the way.

Cathy's body lost its balance. It fell on top of her head, lost the axe amidst the heaped meat, then rolled harmlessly off to one side.

Cathy slowly raised her body back onto its knees. It began feeling around, searching for the axe. This was hard going, as the weapon had fallen out of the head's range of vision. Behind the head, the body felt around blindly.

"Hey—pay attention to *me* for a minute," Amy told Cathy.

Cathy stopped concentrating on her body and focused on Amy. "Hey, you're wearing my clothes! How dare you touch my things? I'm gonna—"

"Shut up, kid—that's not the point here. Me wearing your clothes is currently the least of your worries. Just listen to me."

Cathy glowered at her, but kept silent.

Amy smiled. "See, I know you can heal yourself if you're wounded, little girl, but I don't think you can rebuild a head from scratch if you don't have one. And in about ten seconds after this conversation ends, you ain't gonna have one." She paused for dramatic effect. "Do you understand me, kid?"

Cathy did. "No!" she gasped in horror. "No, don't you dare do it!"

"Sorry, teenage rampage, but for you, the party just ended."

Amy stepped back, took careful aim at the severed blue head with the red horns and pleading eyes and screaming mouth, and pulled the trigger.

The Remington 870 boomed like thunder. Cathy's head exploded into what must have been a thousand pieces.

Amy spat down into the space it had occupied. "Like I said earlier, I'm Amy Fox. I'm a total badass bitch and this is *my* damn revenge party." She paused a moment, then added, "And besides, you should be thanking me, girl. I just ended your fashion violation issues—or where the hell were you planning on going in public with a body that color anyway?"

Cathy's decapitated body now jerked upright and began shambling aimlessly about the barn. Amy leaned against the workbench and watched it roam. She figured Cathy's head had less chance of reconstituting itself than one had of finding a virgin in an abortion clinic—there wasn't anything left of it but a few scraps of blue meat and some chips of red stone that must have come from her horns.

By sheer chance, Cathy's body missed walking into the demon plants. Which made Amy wonder what to do about the plants.

The nasty things had to be destroyed, but how?

Then she remembered the chainsaw she'd heard on rousing after being knocked out.

She looked around for it. It was on a wood stump behind the workbench, its blade slick with the gore from its last two victims. After putting down the shotgun, she picked it up and pulled the starter cord.

The chainsaw first coughed as though unwilling to help her perform her intended task, then it roared to life, its long blade casting chunks of torn flesh at the floor.

Amy headed towards the black plants.

At first the plants tried to attack her. They flung their dark tentacles at her and tried to wrap them around her. This was how she discovered that the tentacles had sharp hooks on them, when they brushed against her skin and tried to snare her.

But then the plants realized that she wasn't like either Sylvia or Ronan who hadn't put up any resistance. Amy was armed and dangerous. The chainsaw sliced through the rubbery tentacles with the ease of a finger being pulled through water.

After that the plants leaned away from Amy, while she, confident but realizing that she really only had the element of surprise on her side, pressed her advantage to the maximum. Amy understood that the demon plants couldn't defend against her simply because she was something new to their experience—she was 'food' which fought back. But she also knew that sooner or later their very desperation to escape her onslaught against them might trigger a counterattack.

The black demonic plants rustled and shook and trembled and shrilled like intelligent things.

And died. Yes, they died.

Exhibiting an instinct for survival, the plants tried to flee. While the eyes in their borrowed faces bulged in a crazed approximation of fear, the plants tried to escape their metal tubs, pulling themselves up with roots which were in reality human hands. But their efforts were futile. The two or three that managed to climb out of their tubs instantly fell over and were unable to get up again. Human hands might make good roots for demon trees, but they were never designed for locomotion.

Amy cut them all down, butchering them with almost inhuman savagery, passing the chainsaw blade through fat black stalk after fat black stalk, through friend's face after friend's face, grinning as the plants ejected their dark sap then withered.

Demon plants? Amy harvested them all like a demoness reaper. They quivered before her like wheat before a sickle, like human souls before Death.

Finally it was over. She stood sweating, her breasts heaving. She was covered in black muck, her silver hair now dyed black. The chainsaw hummed in her grasp.

But the evil flesh-eating plants were all empty sacks now, deflated and lifeless. They were like balloons that had been filled with gaseous hatred, and once that repellent air had been let out of them, they'd returned to being empty nothings.

Amy waited a couple of minutes, to ensure the plants wouldn't make some kind of a comeback, then she switched off the chainsaw.

Her plant-destroying odyssey had taken her across to the far side of the barn. She set the chainsaw down on a stack of pallets, then sat beside it to catch her breath. She felt satisfied that she'd ended a great evil. But she wasn't pleased. There had been too much bloodshed, too much murder.

Alright, she thought, *what now?*

That question was answered for her when, peering out of the nearest barn window, she saw a ridiculously tall black figure step out from the woods.

She felt a thrill of terror. *Shit, he's back!*

Amy didn't know what the TALL man would do once he found out that she'd killed his plants, but she was certain neither shotgun nor chainsaw would be much defense against him if he got violent with her.

He was coming fast now, covering much distance with his impossibly wide strides.

Amy Fox, you'd better get the hell out of Dodge City!

That decided, Amy leapt to her feet and ran across the barn. After picking up the shotgun, she climbed out of the window directly opposite the one through which she could see the giant man approaching. Then she ran into the sunflower field.

Once concealed among the sunflowers, she paused for a moment to get her bearings, then, keeping her head down, headed in the direction of the three smaller barns near the farmhouse.

Meanwhile, back in the old barn, Cathy's headless body had now arrived at the front wall and was trying to walk through it.

CHAPTER 60

Amy

Amy cut past the farmhouse. While casing the distant barn earlier in the day, she'd noticed a shortcut that ran from behind the barns to the meandering road that lead to the state highway.

Once she'd reached that road, she felt much safer. She relaxed and walked slower. Now shock began setting in as a delayed reaction to what she'd experienced. And along with her shock came disbelief.

Only now, after defeating her fears, did she truly begin to feel terrified.

How in the hell? What the hell?

Questions; no answers.

Somewhere along the way Amy remembered she'd not cocked the Remington again after blowing Cathy's head apart. She did so now, the metallic click and zing as the shell ejected from the chamber bringing her alert again.

She wasn't expecting any more danger, but if there was she'd be ready. She was certain the tall man hadn't noticed her escape.

He's likely still trying to figure out what happened to his precious plants, and to Cathy and Ronan. So, I've got a few minutes head start. Once I hit the highway—

She heard the sound of a car approaching and ducked back into the woods. Then, seeing it was a police squad car, she stepped out of hiding and flagged it down.

The car pulled over to her. The officer was young, with brown hair and gray eyes that narrowed suspiciously on seeing the shotgun she carried and the disarray she was in.

"What happened to you?" he enquired.

"I . . . I . . ." Amy discovered she couldn't reply. She didn't know what to say. Now that she was faced with explaining what had happened, it all seemed too ridiculous to relate to a third party.

Instead, she flung down the shotgun and sank to the ground, sitting on the roadside grass. She'd just realized that in her hurry to escape the barn she'd forgotten to take Michael's phone with its video evidence. She grimaced in disgust at her oversight. "Officer, you'd never believe me in a hundred years. Right now I'm trying to convince myself that I ain't crazy. Just get me out of here."

The cop got out of his squad car and came and helped her up. He got her standing upright. She leaned against him, trembling with released emotion.

"I'd better call for backup," he said.

"Don't bother, man, around here the phones don't work."

"Yeah," he replied in an amused voice, "they don't. And do you know why that is? It's because I placed a shield over this farm."

It took a few seconds for the import of his words to reach her, then she jerked back and took a proper look at him.

"Nooooooo!" she moaned.

It was him, the impossibly tall man, so tall that her head didn't even reach his waist. What she'd been leaning against, imagining it was his entire body, was actually just his right leg. She gaped about in confusion.

Where's the car!? Where's the squad car!? her mind queried wildly.

But there was no police cruiser in the road. The road was empty. Whatever she'd seen had never really been.

"Sorry, lady, but I can't leave any witnesses behind," the Bargainer said. "No one must ever know I was here. And you're guaranteed to say something about this once you're under the influence of drugs again."

And with that, he grabbed hold of Amy's head in both giant hands and began squeezing.

The head pressure hit Amy like the world's greatest migraine.

"NO! NO! STOP IT!" she screamed.

Amy fought desperately to squat and reach the Remington; the tall man's crotch was perfectly positioned for her to blast his testicles off. But he had too firm a grip on her head.

The Bargainer squeezed harder, his giant hands completely enclosing Amy's head. There was some slight resistance and then Amy

Fox's skull caved in. Her head popped like a pimple, shooting her brain skyward in a pink and red mess.

Dragging her corpse after him by its silver hair, the Bargainer strolled over to where her brain had landed. He picked Amy's brain up, stuffed it into her tee shirt so it looked like she now had three breasts, then hauled her off through the woods, towards the distant old barn.

CHAPTER 61

The Bargainer

The Bargainer dropped Amy's corpse on the bloody workbench. He forgot about it. With no plants to feed, he had no need to chop her up.

Before hurrying off to waylay Amy Fox, the Bargainer had already taken stock of the situation. Now he took action.

Here in the barn he was just seven feet tall. Shortening himself made getting around easier.

He swore under his breath at the wreckage of Underboss's demon plants. Underboss would be upset about this. It had really wanted the creepy things to produce their crop.

The Bargainer had already determined Ronan's demise from an uneaten horn and several unconsumed shreds of clothing lying amongst the destroyed plants. He shook his head. *I warned the man to be careful around the creepy things. And, just look at his daughter too . . .*

But then the Bargainer's wrinkled face creased up even more in a cold, cold smile.

Oh no, it wasn't a complete waste.

I played the game of odds smartly this time and it worked out just fine.

He strode down to the foot of the barn, where Cathy Higgins' body was still marching forward at the wall. Devoid of mental control, the headless blue form kept bumping into the wall, bouncing back again, and then repeating the same mistake over and over.

The Bargainer grabbed hold of the body, turned it around, and steered it back up to the workbench. After taking a second to tumble Amy Fox over onto the pile of shredded meat, he lifted Cathy's remains up there instead. Her body kept trying to leave the table though, so, while searching through his jacket pockets, he held it down with a firm hand on its belly. The headless corpse still squirmed, but now that it was lying on its back, it no longer had any traction for its feet.

The Bargainer found what he was looking for, a long and empty transparent jar with a rubber stopper. He unstopped the jar, then still holding the girl's body down, he pulled up her dress with his free hand, noted that she wasn't wearing panties, spread her piebald thighs and placed the bottle's mouth firmly against her sky-blue sex.

Then he pressed very hard on her belly. The response was almost immediate: a writhing sludge of pink worms and blue jelly squirted out of her vagina into the jar between her legs.

The Bargainer pressed two more times before deciding he'd emptied her.

Then, after letting her body down from the workbench to stagger aimlessly about again, he examined what he'd collected.

It wasn't really worms, he knew. Worms didn't have arms and legs and apelike faces which even at this fetal stage of their development seemed sour with bad intent. Nor did worms have teeth like shiny metal hooks.

But what the things squirming in the jar *were*, that the Bargainer didn't know. Underboss had been cagey about the second batch of seeds it had given him. All it had told the Bargainer was to, "place them in the womb of a young human female, preferably one not yet in her twentieth year. If the demon-crop fails, I'll accept this one as a substitute payment."

The Bargainer had complied. Slipping the seeds into Cathy's body after her death had been easy: Loving father that he was, Ronan hadn't wanted to look at his naked daughter's genitals, and so, while helping hold the girl's legs apart, he'd respectfully shut his eyes. The Bargainer had used the opportunity to 'plant' the seeds in Cathy's womb. Then he'd plugged her womb and sex up with the rejuvenating jelly. The jelly had both kept the seeds inside Cathy's body and helped awaken her faster.

Had Cathy not 'died' now, a simple trip to the bathroom would have served to harmlessly flush her out. No hurt would have come to the girl. He really had meant to take she and her father back to the Static Earth with him like he'd promised after their unexpected transformations.

The Bargainer always tried to keep his word. Yes, he was totally amoral, but to him a deal was a deal.

Now, the Bargainer stared once more at his strange harvest, pondering the specific calamities these little segmented horrors in the jar would wreak on the Static Earth once fully grown.

Then he shrugged. A deal was a deal and this one was complete.

He packed the jar away again.

Alright, time to clean up.

He wondered what to do with Cathy's body. Chop it up or take it back home with him and discard it there? It wouldn't be a problem if she wasn't piebald blue all over.

He decided to leave it behind. Here—the Spinning Earth—could do with a few puzzles to ponder.

The demon plants were no problem. They were already withered, would all liquefy in an hour or less.

Which left just the meat pile itself. Soon, at the latest tomorrow morning when Ronan's farmhands showed up to work, the police were going to overrun this place. What to do about that?

Then he burst out laughing. Actually, there was really no problem at all. None whatsoever.

Still laughing, the Bargainer left the barn.

CHAPTER 62

Re-Vanni

Once back in the daylight, the Bargainer strolled across the sunflower fields, down towards the pond.

He arrived at the placid body of water just as the red rowboat arrived at its near shore.

He reached down into the boat and lifted out the woman lying there.

He gently set Vanni Warren down on her feet. She was covered in mud and blue goop and dust, but was unharmed. She grinned up at him, her eyes alight with the glow of insanity.

He regarded her with some regret. A truly beautiful woman, but one now destined for the nuthouse with a 'Never Ever Let Out Again,' stamp on her case file.

"Hey, hey, really tall man," Vanni said, her eyes sparkling up at him, "you know, I saw monsters—real monsters. Big nasty monsters. Yeah, they were black and hot and were frying tomatoes in their eyes. But I killed three of 'em, ya know! Then there was a fat blue one too. Bastard lost his head over me—ha ha!" She beat her breasts with pride. "I'm hotter than the hot monsters. Ya know? Ya know?"

He smiled down at her. "Yeah, I do know, lady. And you know what else I know?"

"What?"

He bent and whispered softly in her ears: "There's more monsters hiding in that barn over there." He pointed to the distant barn.

Vanni frowned at him, confused and upset by the news. "There are?"

The Bargainer nodded. "Yes, lady, there are. Some blue ones too. They're scared of you though; they think you're gonna kill 'em all. So you know what they've done?"

"What?" Her body had now tensed up.

He winked like a conspirator. "They're all pretending to already be dead."

"Ooooh," Vanni said, her eyes widening. "That's really sneaky."

"Yeah, some of 'em have even chopped themselves up to deceive you. They look like raw meat, but they ain't—they're just waiting to bite you to death, to rape and smother you in your sleep." He winked again. "But I know you're a whole lot smarter than that, right?"

"Yes, I am," she growled back at him, a look of purpose settling over her dirty features. "Those monsters can't fool me!" She reached down into the red rowboat and retrieved her machete.

"Look, I gotta run," she told the Bargainer, then set off without looking back.

"Hey, lady, where you goin'?" he called after her.

"I've got business to take care of in that damn barn," Vanni yelled back at him without stopping. She looked every inch the vengeful vixen.

"What kinda business would that be now?"

"I'm off to kill the little bits that the monsters have chopped themselves into. Then I'll kill those smaller pieces too, until I'm certain there aren't any more monsters left hiding inside them. Then I'll kill everything else in there too. Just to make sure."

"Great, great. You'll find some other tools in there. There's a chainsaw and several axes too. There's also a shotgun. There's spare shells for it in a pair of jeans on the floor near the workbench."

"Thanks. I'll make sure to use 'em all. Particularly the shotgun, to keep intruders away."

"Which reminds me, lady . . ." She was quite a distance away now, so he had to shout. "One or two of the monsters may even pretend to be cops!"

Her fading voice came floating back over the blossoms. "Gotcha, tall guy! Thanks for the heads up!"

"Yeah," the Bargainer mused to himself as Vanni vanished completely beneath the glorious carpet of sunflower blooms. "Crazy logic, but nonetheless effective."

That was taken care of then. He predicted that, working with an incensed and insane zeal, she'd tire herself out chopping the meat into smaller and smaller pieces; not to mention those two whole bodies in there. Then she'd fall asleep and resume work in the morning. She was certain to still be chopping up her delusional 'monsters' when the farmhands and police arrived.

Vanni would get the blame for everything. The initial police assumption would be that she ran amok on the partygoers and butchered them all. Of course, once the police investigated, they'd know she'd not done it. Particularly since a lot of body parts—in some cases, whole people—would be missing. But with no other suspects, and Vanni crazy to boot and unable to defend herself . . .

Enter yet another padded cell resident.

"Yeah, it wraps up nicely like that," the Bargainer said.

He looked around the farm one last time, trying to remember if he'd overlooked anything.

No, I don't think I have. Time to go home.

But then he did remember something:

Before leaving the Higgins Farm for good, the Bargainer remembered to unblock all the telecoms coverage over it.

Then he walked off, taller than the trees and slowly seeming to fade into them, as if he were merely a figment of this Earth's imagination.

But on Earth's dark and evil twin, he was real, real, real.

The End.

ABOUT THE AUTHOR

Wol-vriey is Nigerian, and quite tall.

He believes there actually are things that go bump in the night.

He writes horror fiction—for adults only, please. And also some surrealist stuff.

Wol-vriey blogs at: *http://oddityfarm.wordpress.com*

WOL-VRIEY
BIZARRO AND TRANSGRESSIVE FICTION

BOSTON POSH (BUD MALONE #1)

In 2028 AD, the USA is a nation ravaged by hungry dragons and dinosaurs. In Boston, Massachusetts, private eye Bud Malone is hired to rescue a kidnapped heiress. But nothing is as it seems.

Malone works to unravel a tangled web involving Boston Chinatown, a 200-year-old woman with a 9-year-old body, white robots, a human-liver-eating psychopath, a golem, a porcelain dragon, and a snake goddess with a crush on him. There's also a woman obsessed with chicken sex. Then Malone meets Posh Lane, a gorgeous call girl who's desperate to quit her pimp.

Romantic sparks ignite between Posh and Malone, but Posh's past suddenly catches up with her in a BIG way. To save Posh, Malone agrees to run a quest for Earth's new rulers, the Forks. But, Malone has no idea that agreeing to the Fork's odd request will send him on the weirdest trip he's ever been on in his life.

BOSTON CORPSE (BUD MALONE #2)

MAGIC CAN BE MURDER! - Drag queen Lucy Tang is back in Boston, and is hell-bent on settling her vindetta against casino owner Sookie Ling. And suddenly, Bud Malone, PI, has the case of his life to resolve.

When Boston's robot police force are baffled by a mind transfer case, they come to Malone for help. The one person who can likely help Malone out here is the witch Soledad Bathory. But Soledad seems to know a lot more than she's telling him. It's a case not made easier when Malone meets Soledad's beautiful cousin, Josephine 'Slave' Bailey. Slave has her own plans for Malone, most of which involve teaching him BDSM and making him her new Master.

Oh, and Rick Rogers owes Sookie Ling a whole lot of money, a gambling debt that's going to be literally Hell to pay!

BOSTON CORPSE - Not your average detective novel!

Burning Bulb
PUBLISHING

WOL-VRIEY
BIZARRO AND TRANSGRESSIVE FICTION

BOSTON LUST (BUD MALONE #3)

"Bless it, Father, for she has sinned."

Seven murdered gay women, all their bodies completely drained of blood. All also with large parts of their bodies dissolved away like acid has been pumped into their veins.

Bud Malone has to find the female vampire preying on Boston's lesbian population.

Then Malone meets the beautiful Trudi Carmen and the case gets even more tangled. Trudi needs Malone's help in recovering a ring that's gone missing. But how in the world is one little black ring related to either the dead women or their killer?

Resolving this case will lead Malone deep into Lucy Tang's legacy—The Abstracta. And then to the city of Genesis.

Boston Lust—Just when you thought Bean Town was safe to visit again.

HELL DANCER

Six people find themselves trapped in Detention, a nightmare realm where the demonic Schoolmaster is hell-bent on reforming them . . . until they die.

Porn superstar Venus Deluxe came to Springfield, MA to party, and next found her life hanging by a thread. One wrong answer will mean her death.

Suspended BPD detective Tanya Rockford was trying to stop one kind of violence, but found a terrifying another. With her and her companion's lives hanging in the balance, it's going to take all of her courage and resourcefulness to escape this hell she's stumbled into.

Porn stud Chad Cannon has made a career from his ten-inch penis. Here in Detention, however, it's his brains that matter. He'll soon be hoping all the pot he's smoked over the years hasn't completely messed up his memory.

The three students, Sherri, Jordan, and Mike? They were all just in the wrong place at the right time. Will anyone survive Detention? The evil Schoolmaster doesn't plan on letting that happen . . .

Burning Bulb
PUBLISHING

WOL-VRIEY
BIZARRO AND TRANSGRESSIVE FICTION

VAGINA MUNDI

Rachel Risk is a professional thief with super-strong hair that can stretch like tentacles to manipulate objects. Ashley Status has both a digitally augmented brain, and 'muscle-purses' in her arms and legs in which she stores inflatable objects—cars, guns, rocket launchers, etc.

When Raye is framed as the fall girl in a jewel robbery, the pair flee Chicago's vengeful robot gangsters and take refuge in the Hotel Bizarre, where the gorgeous 'vagina singer,' Femina, is performing for a week.

But the Hotel Bizarre is even stranger than its name suggests, and very soon Raye and Ash are involved in an deadly adventure, a struggle for survival the likes of which they'd never imagined possible—with loads of deviant sex, drugs, music, and violence at every turn. And just what is the old woman in the skin desert really doing with all those cats glued to her walls?

VAGINA MUNDI—a Bizarro Hymn in praise of WOMAN!

VEGAN VAMPIRE VAGINAS

The biggest bank heist in US history. And Tom Palmer can't remember pulling it off. And no, this isn't your standard case of amnesia. After a one-night-stand gone horribly wrong, Boston salesman Tom Palmer wakes up with a vagina implanted in his left hand. Then his day gets worse.

Tom is transported across space-time to a nightmare version of Boston, one where the Bizarro virus has transformed half the population into cannibals. Worst of all, Tom discovers that in this new Boston, he's the infamous gangster Pussypalm, wanted for robbing the Federal Reserve Bank of Boston a year ago. He also learns that the vagina in his hand is prophetic, i.e. it talks . . . after sex.

With 130 people left dead during his bank heist and six billion dollars missing, Tom knows he's living on borrowed time. It is in his best interests not to remember anything. Because once he does . . .

Burning Bulb
PUBLISHING

WOL-VRIEY
BIZARRO AND TRANSGRESSIVE FICTION

VEGAN ZOMBIE APOCALYPSE

In the post-apocalypse worlderness, zombies rule the earth. They're allergic to meat, and brains literally make them explode. Zombies now eat blood potatoes, parasitic tubers grown in the flesh of humancows corralled in maximum security farms. Two fugitives meet in the ancient ruins of Texas. The first is Soil 15-f, a womancow who's escaped her farm a week before she's due to be killed and her blood potato crop harvested. The second fugitive is Able Kane, former head necros food technician, now sentenced to death for heresy. But Soil is no ordinary humancow.

Unknown to herself, she's the vegan zombie agricultural revolution, and the zombies desperately want her back. And the necros equally desperately want Able Kane dead. He's fled with a forbidden discovery which will reshape the world for the worse if used. And Able is just hardheaded/misguided enough to use it.

MELANIE NEMESIS CATCHPOLE

In Springfield, Massachusetts, Melanie Catchpole is hired to fetch back a magic teddy bear worth millions of dollars from a warehouse across town. Problem is, the warehouse is down in Springfield's O-Zone—that totally weird sector of the city where Bizarro fell to Earth. The 'O' is a fairytale land, a place where dreams and nightmares literally live and breathe..

Worse still, the gingers—mutant cannibals—prowl the O. The gingers have already eaten everyone else Melanie's employers sent to get back the magic teddy bear.

Accompanied by the handsome but ruthless Doug Fisher (who she finds sexy but doesn't dare entrust her heart to), Melanie enters the O-Zone. Melanie and Doug are instantly caught up in an adventure they'd never have believed credible even if written as fiction . . . and Melanie's used to experiencing the very weird as the norm.

And now, additionally, there's a mystery to unravel: What does the dark, freezing-cold being called The Fixer want with Mary, the barkeep's daughter?

Burning Bulb
PUBLISHING

WOL-VRIEY
BIZARRO AND TRANSGRESSIVE FICTION

BIG TROUBLE IN LITTLE ASS

From Bizarro master storyteller Wol-vriey comes a truly weird western tale that will leave you awe-struck and on the edge of your seat...

In the town named Little Ass, tight-assed prostitute Rosa overhears a gunslinger's plans to assassinate rancher Edison Bennett. Once the badass Bennett learns of the plot, he ensures there'll be hell to pay for any attempt on his life!

Yes, it's going to take all of gunslinger Jude's shooting prowess, his eclectic collection of strange firearms, a trusty horse that requires an owners' manual, and the help of the lovely and invigorating Nell (who's EXTREMELY odd when the going gets weird), to survive the Bizarro hell that Edison Bennett unleashes in order to hold onto the land that he'd stolen from Madam Zizi.

BIZARRO 101 (A BASIC PRIMER)

Welcome to the strange place:

A collection of 37 flash fiction stories designed to introduce one to the Bizarro/New Weird Genre.

Weird, dreamy, nightmarish, absurd, sad, surreal, humorous . . . this collection of tales is all this and more.

***

"This primer is the very essence of any and all styles and types of Bizarro writing. Wol-vriey collects, distills, and bottles up these 37 tiny stories for your sensory enjoyment. This is an absolute must-read for anyone new to the genre, because it demonstrates the scope of what Bizarro is, and what it can be."
—Teresa Pollack, Bizarro commentator and blogger

Burning Bulb
PUBLISHING

WOL-VRIEY
BIZARRO AND TRANSGRESSIVE FICTION

Dr. Orgasm

Courtney Taylor is young, intelligent, beautiful, and successful. She also has a boyfriend who loves her deeply. The problem is, no matter what Courtney does, she can't climax during sex.

When Florence Rigid's communist forces destroy the city of Metaphor, Courtney and her friends Teresa, Highball, Miki, and Heather are cast into the midst of a quest to find the only person able to save the land of Innuendo—Dr. Carol Orgasm, wanted by the communists for developing the O-Pill, a wonder drug that grants women sexual ecstasy on demand.

The communists will do anything to get their hands on the O-Pill and prevent its reaching the millions of Innuendo's women. But Courtney desperately wants that pill too. And so it's now a race between Courtney and the communists to find Dr. Orgasm first.

And Courtney has no choice but to win this race. She must win it: For her own orgasm . . . and for the freedom of female sexuality everywhere.

PUSSY TRANSMISSION

Pussy Transmission were the most decadent Pop Art ensemble of the 90's. Led by the beautiful painter Isis Lynch, the trio revolutionized the art world. Then suddenly, without explanation, Pussy Transmission vanished into historical obscurity. Now, twenty years later, three women come to Lynch Place. Lily and Nina are journalists desperate to interview Isis Lynch. Raven, on the other hand, wants to find her boyfriend, who's gone missing inside Isis's house. Raven's worried—she's heard that Pussy Transmission broke up because Isis began dabbling in black magic . . . with devastating results. All three women will shortly wish they'd never left home. Particularly once the rats in Lynch Place start warning them that they're going to die . . . and Raven meets Betty Butcher, the bouncy supernatural psycho who's intent on chopping her into bits. Pussy Transmission, Baby! Just because . . .

Burning Bulb
PUBLISHING

WOL-VRIEY
BIZARRO AND TRANSGRESSIVE FICTION

GIRLS ARE NOT SMILING

Welcome To The Road Trip From Hell

Pagan is demon-possessed.

Lori is suicidal.

Britt is just terminally pissed off.

Meet three young Boston women on the run from the law, each with problems that will fuse into more than the sum of their individual parts, becoming a holocaust of sex and violence and terror, a literal rain of blood and horror and gore and evil.

And if that wasn't already bad enough, Pagan's pet demon is slowly transforming her into something both unspeakable and unholy. Truly, these girls aren't smiling.

BLUE NIGHTMARES

Consummate EVIL is coming. It is relentless and unavoidable. It is Blue.

Jessica Schreiber is seeing things. Very horrible things. Since arriving in Raynham for what should have been a relaxing vacation, she's been seeing *The Big Blue*.

Jessica is smelling things too—dead and rotting things that she can't see. She is sure those dead and rotting things are dead people. Lots of dead people.

Jessica's worst nightmares will soon become her reality. Her reality will soon become a terrifying nightmare.

The tentacled residents of the House of Death have a lot that they wish to show Jessica Schreiber. They have a lot that they wish to tell her. But will she survive long enough to learn their lessons?

Burning Bulb
PUBLISHING

WOL-VRIEY
BIZARRO AND TRANSGRESSIVE FICTION

BRAINCHEW

It was supposed to be a simple jewel heist, but it went badly wrong. Chuck got shot and died.

Lance hid his friend's corpse in the Pleasant Street Cemetery. But that was a big mistake—there was something undead, something extremely hungry . . . something eXXXtremely horrible, buried in the Pleasant Street Cemetery.

And Lance had just woken it up.

They called the monster Brainchew because it ate brains. Human brains. And it preferred those brains fresh from the heads . . . of the living.

And now it was awake again, Brainchew planned on feeding big-time tonight. Oh hell yes, it did.

BRAINCHEW 2: OUT OF THEIR HEADS

After Tiff Hooper recognizes Josh Penham, the man who abducted her and kept her in his basement and abused her, she brings her three friends to Raynham for a night of well-deserved revenge on him.

Only things don't go according to plan.

It is never a good idea to leave a corpse in Raynham's Pleasant Street Cemetery. You run the very real risk of awakening what lies underground there. And that thing—Brainchew—is more horrible and more evil than anything the average mind conceives of even in its worst nightmares.

Brainchew is back! And this time the monster is extra-hungry. But there are plenty of delicious human brains about tonight, and Brainchew intends to eat them all before dawn.

Burning Bulb
PUBLISHING

WOL-VRIEY
BIZARRO AND TRANSGRESSIVE FICTION

DARIA: AN EROTIC NIGHTMARE

Even the best laid women can go wrong.

Daria Simpson is HUNGRY. She's HUNGRY for sex and bloodshed and death.

Shelly Parker just wanted to have a threesome with her boyfriend Craig and her best friend Erica. Everything was shaping up nicely for their weekend of sexual fun and games, until they stopped at the creepy Crossway Diner and met Daria.

From the moment they met Daria, EVERYTHING went wrong for them; and it went wrong in the most horrific and terrifying of ways!

Daria: Paranormal service has been resumed.

WET BONES

Greg is about learning the hard way that you don't mess with Aunt Grace.

Nine completely fleshless skeletons recovered in the Massachusetts woods. Two detectives on the trail of a horrible, hungry monster.

Broken-hearted Allie Jackson has a date with a creature from Hell.

Things are about to get well out of hand for everyone, and in horrifying, terrifying ways they don't expect.

Burning Bulb
PUBLISHING

WOL-VRIEY
BIZARRO AND TRANSGRESSIVE FICTION

MR. UGLY

When a rotting corpse appears and starts butchering Raynham's youths, there's really only one question that needs answering:

Is this faceless and rotting monster Peter Howard, or isn't it?

Problem is, Peter Howard died 15 years ago. So how can he possibly be back from the dead and murdering people with such relentless and incredible brutality?

Peter's mother Malicia, who's just been released from the lunatic asylum may have the answers to the crazy puzzle, but the two detectives investigating the deaths don't even know the right questions to ask her yet.

BRUTAL

Jane Winters is 28 years old.

She works as a checkout cashier in a department store. She's an attractive woman with a winning personality. She has both a photographic memory and an I.Q. of 189.

She's met the man of her dreams.

But she's also a cannibal with a unique and very scary mode of operation.

The group known as TULIP (The Urban Legend Investigation People) are out to either prove or disprove the legend of Insane Jane.

But have TULIP bitten off more than they can chew?

Burning Bulb
PUBLISHING